TRIAL LOVE

TRIAL LOVE

Elizabeth Tettmar

Chivers Press ● G.K. Hall & Co.
Bath, England   Thorndike, Maine USA

This Large Print edition is published by Chivers Press, England, and by G.K. Hall & Co., USA.

Published in 1998 in the U.K. by arrangement with Severn House Publishers Ltd.

Published in 1998 in the U.S. by arrangement with Chivers Press, Ltd.

U.K. Hardcover ISBN 0–7540–3421–6 (Chivers Large Print)
U.K. Softcover ISBN 0–7540–3422–4 (Camden Large Print)
U.S. Softcover ISBN 0–7838–0249–8 (Nightingale Series Edition)

The text of this Large Print edition is unabridged.
Other aspects of the book may vary from the original edition.

Set in 16 pt. New Times Roman.

Printed in Great Britain on acid-free paper.

British Library Cataloguing in Publication Data available

Library of Congress Cataloging-in-Publication Data

Tettmar, Elizabeth.
    [Nurse on approval]
    Trial love / Elizabeth Tettmar.
      p. cm.
    Originally published under the title: Nurse on approval and
      pseudonym Jennifer Eden.
    ISBN 0–7838–0249–8 (lg. print : sc : alk. paper)
    1. Large type books. I. Title.
    [PR6070.E86N87 1998]
    823'.914—dc21   98–23160

CHAPTER ONE

It was one of those days. It had started badly enough—by six-thirty it was heading for disaster.

Laurie fumbled for her notecase. She was hampered by the laden basket slung over her left arm and nervously aware that the youth behind her was clicking his fingers with impatience. It was one of those rare moments when, the rush-hour pressure having subsided, the booking-hall of the Underground station was comparatively empty—and then Laurie discovered she had nothing smaller than a ten-pound note. The booking-office clerk looked annoyed but said nothing. The youth, however, jostled her purposely.

Laurie eased her basket on to her other arm. She didn't normally take a basket to work, but today she had been to Selfridges food store during her lunch hour, and then, much to her embarrassment, she had been presented with farewell presents from the staff and some of the patients at the Beatrix Morse Nursing Home—and the basket had more than come into its own. She felt another push in the small of her back and glared over her shoulder at the skinhead behind. He glared back with expressionless eyes, then pushed her to one side as he made for the escalators. It wasn't a violent push, but Laurie stumbled and her handbag went flying, scattering its contents as it hit the ground.

She went down on her hands and knees and began to gather up her things. She felt sick in the pit of her stomach at the sordidness of the whole incident, and tears of anger and frustration were not far away. She looked up in time to catch a last glimpse of the youth before he disappeared out of her vision—in time to catch his malicious grin; it was shortly afterwards that she discovered that her wallet was missing.

She pulled herself up to her feet again. Her tights were snagged and there was a large dirt mark on her white raincoat, but these were things she noted without feeling. The shock of her loss numbed her for a second or two. She even stooped, picked up her basket and hooked it over her arm again.

Her wallet had gone! She went through her handbag again—then frantically searched the floor around; her wallet bulging with a month's salary had vanished. She felt the colour drain from her cheeks and her heart skipped sickeningly. That was all the money she had to live on until she found another job, and goodness knew when that would be. Miss Marten had thought it odd when Laurie had insisted on cash instead of a cheque, but Laurie had had her reasons *then*. Now she regretted them. She looked at the empty escalator. There was no sign of the skinhead—he had gone, and her wallet had gone with him.

'Excuse me,' came a crisp voice behind her, 'are you admiring the view, or are you nervous about getting on?'

It wasn't a friendly voice, and the face that went with it didn't look particularly friendly either. Laurie was aware of a pair of keen grey eyes and a lock of dark brown hair falling across a wide, high brow. The man was dressed in smartly cut country clothes.

'Excuse me,' he said again, a little more abruptly, 'but I do happen to be in a hurry—I have another train to catch.'

Not stopping to think, Laurie clutched hold of his arm. 'I've been robbed,' she said, her voice rising with her panic. 'All my money—a month's wages—a horrible-looking youth, a skinhead, pushed against me on purpose and made me drop my handbag, then he snatched my wallet and went off on the escalator. Please help me—you'd catch up with him if you hurried, a train hasn't come in yet. Oh, do hurry—you can't mistake him, he's all dressed in black and got mean little eyes and a skinhead—'

She faltered to a stop, seeing that the man was making no effort to move, but instead was staring at her very steadily.

'You saw him take your wallet?'

'Oh no—but who else could it have been? He pushed against me on purpose—'

3

'And where was your wallet?'

'In my bag. I'd just put it away.' She drew herself up; the feeling of shock and helplessness that had clamped down on her was beginning to lift, and indignation was coming to her aid. 'Who are you to cross-examine me?' she demanded.

He ignored that. 'If you'd put your wallet in your bag, how could this—this young man have snatched it from you without you noticing? You say your bag fell on the ground. Did he bend down and pick anything up?'

Laurie tried to think back. Everything had happened so quickly, and now her head was spinning with the effort of trying to remember. Anyway, what did this stranger mean by trying to make her feel the guilty party!

'No, I don't think he did, but he *must* have taken my wallet—who else could have done so? Besides, he's a—' she stopped herself.

'You were going to say—"Besides, he's a skinhead!" I suppose that automatically makes him out a thief and vagabond as far as you're concerned.'

Colour ran into her cheeks at the look he gave her. 'I didn't say that!'

'You implied it.' His eyes travelled deliberately from her face down to her basket. Without any change in his voice he asked, 'Is that your wallet, lying there on top of your shopping?'

Laurie followed his gaze—and yes, there was

4

her wallet, where it had fallen on the top of a gift-wrapped box of chocolates. She gulped, frightened to raise her eyes and risk another scathing look from this insufferable man.

'I advise you to think carefully in future before you start accusing innocent bystanders of assault and robbery,' he said, making her feel about two inches high. Then he turned on his heel, stepped on the escalator and was mercifully soon out of sight.

Laurie waited a moment or two before following him. A few more passengers had arrived and she made way for them. She had been through so much emotion already that day that this ugly incident was the last straw. She felt tears gush to her eyes and blinked them away. What a fool she had made of herself! She hoped and prayed that his train had already gone.

She saw her train waiting in the station and ran to board it before the doors closed. There was only one seat vacant, and as she lurched towards it the train gathered speed and she almost fell into the lap of the man sitting opposite. She apologised without looking at him, conscious of the tears still hanging to her lashes, and sank thankfully into the empty place. Her legs still felt shaky from her recent encounter—then she looked up, straight into a pair of watching grey eyes.

She tried staring back, but the fire in her azure blue eyes had no effect—if anything it

5

seemed to amuse him, for his lips quirked up into a sardonic smile. Then he grew serious and went very thoughtful, scrutinising her with narrowed eyes as if trying to place her in his memory.

There was something familiar about his face too—but then women's magazines were full of photos of rugged-looking men with deep-set eyes, Laurie told herself. To the best of her knowledge she had never seen him before, and she wished she didn't have to sit looking at him now. She could have got up and walked down the compartment to strap-hang near the door, but that would have conceded victory to him, and her pride wouldn't allow that. She had a stubborn chin which she had a habit of jerking in the air when her back was up. She could see herself reflected in the window opposite, and thought how prim she looked with her black, shoulder-length hair strained back from her face and tied at the back—a convenient style for work. Off duty she wore her hair loose as it gave fullness to her face, softening the curve of her cheek. She was not pretty in the conventional sense, but she had her attractive points, such as her dimples and the long sweep of her black lashes.

She found herself turning hot once more under the constant scrutiny of the man opposite. She tried reading all the adverts, but she knew them by heart already, and anyway she knew that by trying to look casual she might only succeed in looking selfconscious. She decided to try and stare him out again; she had quashed many an Underground ogler like that during her two years travelling back and forth to the Beatrix Morse. But such tactics were unnecessary. He had suddenly remembered where he had seen her—recognition flared in his eyes and then faded, to be replaced by a complete detachment as if now he knew who she was he was no longer interested. He even got out his paper and began to read.

Laurie seethed with hidden anger. How dared he stare at her like that, then shrug her off as if she were something of no importance! She felt like leaning across and tapping his knee and saying loud enough for the whole compartment to hear:

'I hope you'll know me the next time we have the misfortune to meet!' but was saved from her folly by the train drawing into Liverpool Street. The man folded his paper, put it away, and strode off without giving her another glance. He had completely forgotten her.

By the time the train surfaced into daylight, Laurie had convinced herself that she had also forgotten him—or at least, didn't intend to waste another thought on him. She had things of more importance on her mind. The last month had been a traumatic one for her. She still could not recall without an inner tremor that morning when Miss Marten had called her into her office.

Miss Marten had been under great strain. 'My dear, I wish I didn't have to break this news to you,' she had said. 'But this nursing home is changing hands and the management insists that all staff must be registered. I put in a special plea for you—said what an extremely good nurse you were, that you had only failed one part of your finals and that through extenuating circumstances—but they were adamant. Laurie, wouldn't you consider taking your practical again—for your own sake—for my sake? I don't want to lose you, you're my right hand here.'

Laurie had felt her insides constrict at the very idea.

'I—I can't,' she had whispered. 'You know I can't. It's too long ago—two years—' She didn't want to remember the other reason: that awful day when she was just setting out for the Eastside Hospital to take her practical exam and had received the news that her grandfather was dying.

But the memory would persist, even now in the rattling train. She had stood indecisive, the telephone message in her hands, and it had been Sadie who had fetched a taxi and ruthlessly pushed her into it. 'I'll phone through to Miss Beecher (Miss Beecher was the housekeeper)—tell her you'll go straight from the hospital to see your grandfather. It might be another false alarm, you've had so many. You mustn't miss this exam, Laurie, you owe it to your grandfather. It will mean so much to him to see you qualify. You can't let him down now.'

No, she mustn't do that, she had told herself. He had always been so proud of her—that gentle old man who had been mother and father as well as grandparent. She had been only three when her parents were killed, ironically their first weekend away together since she had been born. She could dimly remember her mother as someone warm and soft to touch and smelling like flowers, and her father as a loud laugh and a pair of strong arms that tossed her up to terrifying heights.

But memories fade, and to the lively three-year old her grandfather became the pivot of her life, and though he ran a busy country practice single-handed he had always found the odd moment for her when she needed him.

The only disappointment she had caused him was chosing nursing instead of medicine as a career. There had been three generations of Bushes at the Eastside Medical School, and he was hoping she would make the fourth, but Laurie knew she was not cut out to be a doctor like her father or his father or his father's father, but nursing appealed to her, and she had appeased the old man by applying to the nursing school at the Eastside Hospital.

She had been a model student, collecting prizes as other girls collected boy-friends. Laurie had no time for boy-friends, she was too busy working. 'Just let me get qualified first,' she would say to Sadie, who couldn't understand such self-denial—she was already engaged, but then Laurie was a girl who never did anything by halves. When she had decided to become a nurse she had also decided to be the best nurse of her year.

And she had nearly achieved it—then her grandfather's health broke up. He had a series of small heart attacks which forced him into early retirement. By this time Laurie was sharing a flat with Sadie Elliott, a school friend and also a student nurse, using it as a kind of bolt-hole on her days off, but after Dr Bush's initial heart attack she had spent all her spare time at his Suffolk home. The strain of dashing off at odd times to make the eighty-mile journey across country began to take its toll. She didn't spare herself and often sat up half the night studying to make up for lost time; by the time her finals came round she felt burnt out—drained of thought and action. Yet she felt she hadn't done too badly in her written work, though she knew it was not the standard to win any prizes. Then the day of the practical—and the telephone message taken by someone in the ground-floor flat.

Even now, as she thought of that time, a kind of paralysis gripped her, shutting off all emotion. She found herself looking at the past as if through the wrong end of a telescope to watch herself, a dwarf-like automaton, walking up the steps of the grim-looking hospital.

She had been the last candidate to be called, and her impatience to get away to her grandfather had mounted as the time had ticked away. At last she was summoned, and blindly stumbled into the ward, her nerves as taut as violin strings. The Nursing Tutor and the Chief Nursing Officer were unknown to her, but their first questions put her at her ease. She had to do a routine examination of a patient, take his blood pressure and temperature and expound on a few basic details. So far no cause for her inner tension to increase. It was only when she was asked to set out an instrument trolley that the first real hiccup had occurred. In her anxiety to get the interview over as soon as possible she was too hasty and dropped a kidney dish; the noise it made echoed through the empty room and she heard an exasperated exclamation from someone in the far corner. She had been aware of a shadowy figure standing there, but had been too occupied to look at him; now when she did she had recoiled from the antagonism in his slate-coloured eyes. After that she had gone completely to pieces—that one look of derision undid all the good that had gone before. Her mind went blank, she couldn't remember even simple things, and when she stumbled against the trolley, sending it flying, she knew that was the end of her finals.

It was an anticlimax to have to go through

the oral—facing her three examiners behind a large table. The man from the shadows had joined his two colleagues to ask her questions, and though he was introduced to her he remained a faceless figure—a symbol of her defeat, a brusque voice and a pair of cold eyes. He put many pertinent questions to her and she couldn't answer one of them. The other two were kinder to her, tried to draw her out, even to make allowances, but the harm had been done. Afterwards she overheard the three of them conferring together. The Nursing Tutor was saying, 'A case of examination nerves—' and brusquely the answer: 'The girl's a fool—wasting our time!' She didn't have to look to see who was speaking.

She was past caring then; the afternoon was drawing to a close and she had to get to Suffolk. She didn't even wait to hear that she had been deferred, she would hear soon enough by post—before dashing out of the hospital and hailing a taxi to take her to Liverpool Street.

It was just turning dusk when she ran up the front path of the yellow brick house on the green. There was no light in her grandfather's room and she took that as a good sign—he must be sleeping, but when the door opened and she saw Beechy's face she knew she was too late. She fell crying into the housekeeper's arms. 'What shall I do without him—oh, Beechy, what shall I do?'

But she had to go on living, and there was so much to do clearing up her grandfather's affairs that she didn't find the time to sit and brood. The estate was straightforward enough; there was very little money. Ill health had prevented Dr Bush earning much in his later years, and he had always been extremely generous. Laurie realised too late the sacrifices he must have made to give her an expensive education and to invest in a small trust fund which would accrue until she was twenty-five. The house and most of the furniture went to Miss Beecher, which was as it should be, as she had looked after him faithfully for nearly thirty years—and her grandfather had expected Laurie to have a husband who would provide a home. The pieces of furniture from her old bedroom and study came to her: a gateleg table, a Chinese rug, a beautifully carved eighteenth-century chair in inlaid rosewood and a set of oak bookshelves. These had been transported to the flat at Woodford—and then at last Laurie was free to review her future.

She had failed her practical. A letter had confirmed this, it also suggested a date for a re-sit. But Laurie now had a complete block as far as her nursing career was concerned—even to think of taking her exam again brought her out in a cold sweat. The events had taken on the aspect of a nightmare, and like a nightmare it seemed shadowy and unreal. She blanked out any thought of turning it back to reality, so she would not even discuss the possibility of a re-sit.

Sadie was scandalised at such a decision. She had qualified as a mental nurse three months earlier. 'What are you doing to do?' she had wailed. 'You don't know anything else *but* nursing!'

Laurie went to evening classes to learn shorthand and typing. Typing came easily to her, but shorthand was always a bugbear, and when she did eventually get a job as a temporary typist she couldn't stand it. Sadie was wiser than she—she knew nursing was in Laurie's blood and that she wouldn't be happy doing anything else. But there was no question of going back to hospital work, she had to be qualified for that, and finally an agency sent her along to the Beatrix Morse Nursing Home in the West End.

It wasn't the kind of nursing she had been used to and she knew experience in general work would be very limited, but she discovered she had a certain knack with sick old ladies, and gradually her busy round of duties helped to erase the hurt of the past six months.

Miss Marten, the Matron, came to rely on Laurie more and more; it was only the fact that she was not qualified that prevented her being promoted to Sister, therefore it had come as a double shock to be told, without any prior warning, that the new management could not renew her contract.

14

And today had been her last day at the Beatrix Morse. Sadie was getting married in two weeks' time and Laurie was determined to take her out over the weekend, buy her a celebration meal and a wedding present of her own choice—that was why she had asked for her month's salary in cash. As to what was going to happen to her now—she shrugged that thought off. She not only had to find another job—but a home as well. They had given in a month's notice on the flat; even in a job Laurie could not have afforded to run it on her own. Sadie and her boy-friend, John Abbott, were both staff nurses at the same hospital and had put a deposit on a small house in the area.

Laurie felt she had been dogged by ill fate to the bitter end, for today had gone wrong right from the beginning. For one thing, Miss Marten had been called away to a conference and she wasn't there to say goodbye; then a new patient had been admitted who threw a tantrum because she didn't like the colour scheme in her room. It had taken all Laurie's tact and patience to win her over; then, just as she was leaving—early as had been arranged because she wanted to get in before Sadie and have supper ready for her—another patient, dear little Mrs Withers, who never before had given any trouble, suddenly went into a fit of vapours.

Laurie had been seriously alarmed at the sight of her and had been about to summon the consultant who was on call, when a querulous voice arrested her. 'I'm not going to stay on here without you, Nurse. I won't like it here without you. You're the only one who has time to sit and talk to me and play cards with me— the others all say they're too busy. If you leave, then so shall I. My daughter-in-law will just have to take me back, that's all. After all, it is my ancestral home she took over.'

Laurie cajoled the old lady into having a hot drink and then sat with her until she was asleep before creeping out of the room. She knew she would be forgotten when Mrs Withers woke up. There was no ancestral home, no daughter-in-law—and now there would be no surprise supper for Sadie either.

The train rattled into Woodford station. Laurie alighted and walked through the streets towards the Green. The flat she shared with Sadie was the converted attic of a late Victorian villa. It was roomy and well lit, but it had its drawbacks; they fried in summer and froze in winter. As compensation they overlooked a boulevard of magnificent horse-chestnut trees which were lit up by their own red candles every spring.

Sadie was already home as she guessed she would be, and the spicy smell of chilli con carne filled the small entrance hall.

'You look absolutely bushed,' was Sadie's greeting. 'Come on, get your feet up and I'll pour you a drink.'

'Not now—later perhaps. Right now I'd love nothing better than a cup of tea, I missed mine this afternoon.'

'Poor you,' said Sadie sympathetically. She was always ready with sympathy, with help, with good advice. She was pretty and plump and dark and had lovely brown eyes. 'I guessed something was up when you weren't in. You said you'd be early—'

While they were in the kitchen waiting for the kettle to boil Laurie recounted some of the events of the day. 'I bought the makings of a pizza and a bottle of Chianti. I wanted to surprise you.'

'Surprise me for lunch tomorrow. What's all that in your basket?'

'Presents. Chocolates and hankies and six bottles of perfume, all different!'

'I'll swap you a toaster for two bottles of scent. I had another one given to me today.'

They giggled across the table at each other—Sadie's wedding presents had been trickling in for the past three months and there was no more cupboard space to hold them, but beneath the surface of Laurie's laughter was a note of desperation and Sadie, detecting it, got to her feet. 'I've got something to show you,' she said. 'But drink your tea first.'

She came back to the kitchen with the evening paper.

'Have you seen this?' she asked.

'No, I didn't stop to buy one, I knew you'd

have a copy.'

'There's a job advertised, Laurie—just up your street!'

Laurie raised reproachful eyes. 'You know the number of jobs I've written after and phoned after and even gone after during the past month, and you know what happens every time I say I'm not qualified.'

'Well, this time don't say it. After all, it was only one small part of your finals you failed. You've been nursing for the past two years, you've got a marvellous record as a student—and what's more, you can do shorthand and typing, which is particularly requested for this job. Here, read for yourself.'

Laurie took the paper with a grudging sigh. She knew Sadie meant well, but at the moment she felt too disheartened and tired to face any more disappointments—and she was certain this would only mean another disappointment. But she didn't even see the advertisement Sadie pointed out; her eyes went to the top of the page and a photograph of four men being interviewed at Heathrow. Underneath the caption read:

Drs Brown, Coupland, Attling and Cramond returning from a Medical Fact-finding Mission in the United States . . .

And it was *him*—the tallest one, the one with

the broad shoulders and the lock of dark hair falling over his forehead. The arrogant one, the one with grey eyes who had slated her in the Underground. Dr Cramond—the name registered now. He was the third examiner—the one in the shadows who had withered her with his cold, calculating stare and made her lose her nerve.

'What are you goggling at?' asked Sadie.

'That's him,' said Laurie, jabbing the paper viciously. 'That's the brute who made me fail my practical. I saw him again today, on the train coming home. I didn't recognise him then, but he recognised me all right, I saw it in his eyes. Oh, if only I'd known who he was, I wouldn't have sat there like a dummy!'

Sadie looked over her shoulder at the paper.

'I rather like that craggy type of face,' she remarked.

Laurie glared, then realised with annoyance that Sadie was teasing. 'You can laugh, but it's no joke. The very sight of him makes my blood boil! Fancy, after all this time, running into him like that. And he was just as objectionable as ever. Oh, how I loathe that man!'

Sadie's smile vanished and she stared at Laurie, concerned. 'Don't you think that's a bit strong? Anyway, how could he possibly have made you fail your practical—and what if he did? Are you going to hold this against him for the rest of your life? I don't *loathe* every examiner who's given me a bad mark, I don't call that very logical.'

'I know, I know—but I *am* illogical, that's one of my faults. And he *did* wreck my self-confidence that day of my practical—it was the way he looked at me, as if he didn't expect me to be any good. Nothing went right for me after that—don't you remember me telling you?'

'You said a lot of things that day,' said Sadie gently. 'You were out of your mind with grief. Then afterwards you wouldn't talk about it at all. But are you sure that this Dr Cramond and the man you said you saw on the train are the same? It's an incredible coincidence.'

'There are no such things as coincidences in my life, there are only disasters, and that man's the biggest disaster of the lot!'

Sadie laughed at that. She had rarely seen Laurie in such a state before, but there was a good side to it—she was now talking freely about the day of the exam. 'All right, I'll take your word for it,' she said placatingly. 'Now let's forget him. Have you looked at the advert yet?'

Laurie had to fold the page over before she could do so. The very sight of Dr Cramond tied her stomach into knots. At first the words danced before her eyes, but as her pulse stopped racing so her mind quietened and she was able to take in what she had read. She read it again—aloud.

. . . Wanted, nurse-receptionist for country practice. Typing essential. Sympathetic manner more important than experience. Please contact Dr Russett for interview. Hotel Parkside—

'There you are!' Sadie broke in triumphantly. 'The job is tailor-made for you. It gives a phone number, so ring now while I dish up supper.'

'I must have a shower first,' said Laurie. 'I didn't even have time for a wash this afternoon.'

'I know what that means—you'll put it off and someone else will nip in and get the job. All right, I'll phone for you.'

When Laurie came out of the bathroom she found a radiant Sadie waiting for her. She was seized round the waist and Sadie danced her along the hall and into the living-room. 'What about this news, my pet, to cheer you up? I've made an appointment for you to see Dr Russett at eleven tomorrow!'

Laurie pulled herself free and stared at Sadie aghast. 'You haven't!'

'Indeed I have. What's more, Dr Russett is a female and sounds an absolute darling. When I said you'd had two years' experience in a private nursing home and had also taken a course in shorthand-typing I could detect her satisfaction oozing down the phone. There is one snag,' Sadie added.

'I knew there would be.'

Laurie looked up to see Sadie laughing at her again. 'The job is in the Cotswolds. I don't suppose you want to bury yourself in the Cotswolds—not after the West End.'

'Stop teasing! You know I'd go anywhere—but that's not the point. It'll be just a waste of time going to this interview. I've only got to say I'm not qualified and that's it, *finis*!'

Sadie didn't bring up the subject again until they had finished supper and were seated in front of the television with cups of coffee on their knees. Thoughtfully stirring, she said, à propos nothing, 'Why bring up the question of qualifications? Go for the interview, play it by ear. If Dr Russett offers you the job grab it, that's my advice. She'll assume that you are qualified, anyway. Afterwards, when you're settled in, tell her if you must. I'm sure when she discovers what a darn good worker you are she won't worry about a missing slip of paper.'

'I think that's the most immoral thing I've ever heard you suggest!' said Laurie hotly. 'That's lying by implication.'

Quite unrepentant, Sadie went on stirring her coffee.

'People out of work can't afford to have scruples,' she said. 'I don't have to remind you of the position you'll be in when I've left and the lease of this flat is up. Where will you go then? I can't see you living on Social Security, so what will you do?'

'I can't act a lie,' Laurie protested.

'You don't have to. Just go for the interview and see what happens. You never know, Dr

Russett may turn out to be another Miss Marten and give you a chance after all.'

Laurie sighed. 'We're both taking it for granted that I'm going to be given this job.'

'You are,' said Sadie.

*   *   *

In spite of her misgivings Laurie was prompt for the interview the following morning, feeling ill at ease in borrowed plumes. Sadie had insisted on lending her a new navy-blue velvet suit for the occasion, far too big, but all objections had been brushed aside with the assurance that it was just the thing for the Parkside Hotel. Fortunately the jacket had dolman sleeves so its looseness did not look out of place, and Laurie was able to gather the skirt in at the waist with a wide belt.

'You look very soignée,' said Sadie, walking round her to see there were no bits sticking to the skirt and ready to attack them with some Scotch tape if there were. 'I hope Dr Russett will be suitably impressed. What a pity she isn't a man.'

'I'm going, before you corrupt me completely,' retorted Laurie, then went back to give Sadie a hug. 'Wish me luck—keep your fingers crossed!'

A pageboy took Laurie up to Dr Russett's room. She turned out to be a short stout woman with a low pleasant-sounding voice, in her late fifties, Laurie guessed. She wore her iron-grey hair unflatteringly short and cut into a fringe across her broad forehead, and she looked Laurie up and down approvingly as she invited her to sit down.

Over coffee she told Laurie about the group practice. There were three partners: herself, a Dr Lawrence and a Dr Ross. Her tone of voice when she referred to Dr Ross, which she did often, was such a mixture of affection and respect that Laurie wondered if her feelings didn't go deeper. She pictured Dr Ross as the senior partner, somebody in his sixties with white hair and a genial manner. She came to to hear Dr Russett talking about Shirley Dickson the dispenser, somebody called Julie and someone else—Pamela Wakefield, the nurse-receptionist, whose job was being advertised. With very little notice her husband had been sent to the Middle East.

'We were going to lose her at Christmas, anyway,' Dr Russett added, relieving Laurie of her cup. 'She's been married for a year and is now expecting her first child. Naturally we understood her wanting to be with her husband, but it put us in a quandary. We've had great difficulty trying to replace her. Suitable applicants didn't want to bury themselves in the country, as so many of them told me; others couldn't type. I gather that is one of your qualifications?'

Laurie nodded, not trusting herself to speak

24

at that moment. Her heart was thudding painfully in anticipation of Dr Russett's next question. But Dr Russett went off on quite a different tack.

'Let's see, if all else is favourable, would you be able to start on Tuesday—Monday being a Bank Holiday?'

Laurie swallowed. 'Y-yes,' she managed to get out.

'Absolutely splendid; I was holding my breath in case you said no. It was a last-minute decision of mine to place that advert in the evening paper—I'd tried everywhere else—and as I was in Town for the holiday weekend catching up on the latest shows, I thought— well, why not—and it's paid off!' Dr Russett's brown eyes twinkled happily at Laurie. 'Now, you'd better tell me something about yourself, my dear. Tell me about the—what was it—' she referred to her diary, 'the Beatrix Morse Nursing Home your friend mentioned.'

Dr Russett was one of those soothing personalities who have the knack of putting people at their ease, and Laurie found herself talking without restraint, even repeating anecdotes about the nursing home that had them both laughing. 'You seem to have been very happy there. What made you decide to leave?' Dr Russett interrupted once.

'This is it,' thought Laurie, her spirits plummeting, 'this is when I see her eyes glaze over.' Then she remembered Sadie's doubtful advice. 'There was a change of management—a different policy—' She stopped, waiting—and as she had hoped Dr Russett rushed in.

'Say no more—it's happening all the time. Cutting down on staff, tightening up on spending—well, all I can say to that is, their loss may be our gain.' She gave Laurie a quizzical look. 'What do you feel about coming into a country practice after working in a fashionable West End nursing home? Did it never worry you, Miss Bush, using your expertise to nurse wealthy hypochondriacs?'

Laurie's face clouded over. 'I never looked on my patients like that,' she said truthfully. 'To me they were just sick people requiring help and I did my best for them.'

Dr Russett's smile came out like a sunburst. 'That was the answer I was praying for,' she said fervently. 'Just a little trick question on my part to test you—forgive me, my dear. Some girls go into private nursing for the money only. I could tell you weren't like that, but I had to make sure. Now let's get down to the sordid business of finance—'

Ten minutes later Laurie was out in the corridor with a cheque to cover advance in salary as well as her fare to Merton-on-the-Hill and accommodation until she found somewhere permanent to live. Still in a daze, she walked right past the lift and came up short by a fire door. She couldn't believe it—she had got a job! She knew Miss Marten would not let

26

her down if she was asked for a reference—everything was going right for her. She turned and walked back to the lift, then stopped again.

Quite unexpectedly an image suddenly appeared before her—an image of a pair of steely grey eyes. She closed her eyes, trying to make the image go away—but there it was superimposed on her inner lids. She knew she could never shut out that look of scorn, it was imprinted on her mind for ever. And if she accepted this job under false pretences, she realised, she would deserve such scorn. That would be putting Dr Cramond in the right—and that she could never do.

With sinking spirits she retraced her steps.

'Come in,' called Dr Russett when she knocked.

CHAPTER TWO

'You've changed your mind,' said Dr Russett, her face dropping at the sight of Laurie. 'It's too short notice.'

'It's not that,' said Laurie with difficulty, then gave the real reason for her return.

The other woman didn't answer immediately, then she smiled—a mere ghost of a smile, but it was sufficient to lift Laurie's spirits.

'Thank you for being honest, I admire you

27

for that. Come and sit down again and tell me all about it.'

For the first time since that awful day Laurie found herself able to talk freely, but she still could not bring herself to mention Dr Cramond and his part in her downfall.

'And you've never once thought about re-sitting your practical?' The doctor's voice held a note of incredulity. 'After your splendid record as a student nurse, I can't understand you not taking the exam again. I'm sure you would have passed it the second time; you were too worried about your grandfather on the first occasion, I can understand that.'

Laurie pleated her handkerchief between nervous fingers. 'I can't explain—it's just that I couldn't even *think* of re-sitting the practical. My mind shied away from it—it was just as if I'd brought down a mental iron curtain. I blotted it out of my memory—I didn't want to remember a single thing that happened to me that day.'

There, it was out at last—something she had not admitted to herself before. And spoken aloud, how foolish and improbable it sounded. But Dr Russett didn't think so.

'Do you know what you're suffering from?' she said gently. 'An enormous guilt complex. Oh yes,' as Laurie made a gesture of disbelief, 'psychology is one of my subjects, so I know what I'm talking about. Shall I explain what happened to you that day? You were torn between going to the hospital and taking your exam and going to Suffolk to see your grandfather. When you failed your practical you looked upon it as a punishment for not being at your grandfather's deathbed. And you won't re-sit the exam because you're still punishing yourself. You've never forgiven yourself for what you consider a lapse of duty, and until you can forgive yourself there will always be this block where your exam is concerned.'

Laurie looked up into the kindly dark eyes and gave a faint smile. 'You make it sound so simple. I wish I could believe it.'

'You can always prove me wrong by just doing nothing, but on the other hand you can prove me right by having another stab at that practical. Look, I'll make a bargain with you. I'll take you on appro for three months if during that time you re-sit your finals. What do you say?'

A great surge of relief brought colour flooding to Laurie's cheeks. 'Oh, gladly, but what about your two partners? Won't they have a say in the matter?'

'Dr Lawrence won't quibble. Dr Ross? Well, he can be difficult at times, but I think I can get round him. His bark is a lot worse than his bite.'

Again Laurie had an image of a benign old country doctor; she would have been stunned if anyone had pointed out that she was trying to

29

resurrect her grandfather. She saw Dr Russett hold out her hand.

'So it's settled, then? Let's shake on it.'

Laurie travelled back to Woodford with her heart singing. The interview with Dr Russett had left her in a glow of optimism. All doubts and fears of the past few years were suddenly lifted. Even thoughts of Dr Cramond faded— exorcised by her new prospects. He was a formless threat now vanquished for ever.

Sadie had lunch ready for her. 'I knew you'd be hungry, you always are in times of crisis. You don't have to tell me you landed your job—I can see it in your face.'

Laurie wasn't usually a demonstrative girl, but now she grabbed Sadie and hugged her until she pretended to squeal with pain. 'Yes, I have got the job, thanks to you,' she cried. 'It's a group practice, with two other doctors besides Dr Russett—Dr Ross, he's the senior and sounds an absolute poppet, and a Dr Lawrence who I gathered is the youngest. And what do you think? They went me to start straight away—Tuesday, so I'll have to travel down on Monday.'

'Oh.' Sadie couldn't hide her disappointment. 'That means we won't have our day in Town together. Never mind,' she added hastily, seeing Laurie's expression change, 'we'll have a get-together some other time.'

Laurie's face clouded over.

'I'm going to miss your wedding too, Sadie. I hadn't thought. I am sorry about that.'

Sadie hooted. 'A good miss that will be—just John and me and two witnesses at the register office; we're not wasting any money on fripperies, we want it for the house. Which reminds me, both John and I have got tomorrow off and I promised I'd help out with some redecorating. I'm sorry, Laurie, I would like to spend the last day with you—everything has happened so quickly at the last minute that I'm beginning to feel giddy.'

Laurie smiled contentedly at her friend. 'I feel giddy too—giddy with relief. I tell you what, I still haven't made you that surprise pizza yet. What about bringing John back here for supper tomorrow night and I'll surprise the two of you!'

But as it happened Laurie did get her day in Town with Sadie after all. She made good use of Sunday, washing and drying and ironing her clothes ready for packing. She had just washed her hair and was sitting at an open window drying it in the sun, when she was called to the communal phone on the ground floor. It was Dr Russett, sounding somewhat distressed. As soon as she recognised her Laurie felt her hopes fall to rock bottom, fearing the worst, but Dr Russett was phoning to say that she couldn't get Laurie fixed up in a local hotel as they were all full owing to the holiday. 'If you could postpone your journey until Tuesday,' she suggested, 'Shirley Dickson, our dispenser, can put you up then, and Dr Lawrence has offered to pick you up at the station.'

Laurie flew back up the stairs with wings on her feet. Not only was her job safe, but her goodbye to Sadie wouldn't have to be rushed after all. She could now take her to London and treat her to that slap-up meal she had been promising her, and to a matinee too if they could get in somewhere.

They were fortunate enough to get two cancellations for the musical at Drury Lane, and later they went to a Chinese restaurant that specialised in Peking-style food so that Sadie could indulge in her liking for crispy duck and fried seaweed. In a gush of sentiment Laurie lifted her glass and drank to Sadie's future happiness. In her more dreamy moods her eyes took on a mauvy tinge. They looked like violets, thought Sadie in an unaccustomed flight of fancy, and her long dark hair shone purple in the subdued lighting. It always amazed her that men didn't flock round Laurie, as she was so attractive, and she had once teased John about it. He had answered in his careful fashion:

'I like Laurie a lot, but she doesn't appeal to me in that way. She's got some sort of barrier up; any chap can sense it and it puts him off. She's one of the old-fashioned sort, waiting for Mr Right. All I hope is that she recognises him before it's too late!'

Tuesday was a misty day with the promise of sun later. Laurie had packed all she could carry into one soft-top suitcase; the rest of her things Sadie would send on later. 'What about your furniture?' she asked. 'Do you want me to put it in store?'

'I don't know. I shall have to wait and see what happens at Merton. If I can manage to get unfurnished rooms, I'd like it with me.'

For travelling she was wearing an overall dress of heavy linen in a natural shade with a roll collar and three-quarter-length sleeves, gathered in at the waist by a wide black patent leather belt. Under it she had on a blue and white check shirt, and her raincoat was strapped to her suitcase for convenience.

'Smart but serviceable,' said Sadie approvingly. She produced a small package. 'Here's a farewell present from John. He was too shy to give it to you personally.'

It was a pure silk pale blue scarf, and Laurie was delighted. 'I'll wear it for luck,' she said, knotting it round her slender throat. The colour enhanced the blue of her eyes, giving them an added depth. The two girls looked at one another for a moment in silence. Sadie couldn't go to Paddington to see Laurie off as she was due to go on duty shortly, so it was an emotional leavetaking in the little flat they had shared since they were students.

'I refuse to say goodbye,' said Sadie, choking back tears. 'John has promise me a short honeymoon, and I'll see to it that we come to the Cotswolds. Can you bear to see a Mr and Mrs so soon after starting a new job?'

'I'd never speak to you again if you didn't come and see me,' retorted Laurie, then she ducked her head and ran, stumbling down the stairs to the front door as if she had roots that were pulling her back.

She was thinking of that now as she travelled deeper into the Gloucestershire countryside, looking out of the train window at the golds and greens and saffron yellow of the gentle hills.

Sadie had been more than a friend; she was some years older than Laurie and had naturally taken on the rôle of an older sister. Certainly she had helped Laurie weather more than one crisis. Laurie sighed. It was a pity in a way that she couldn't have stayed in London, been a neighbour to Sadie and John, even godmother perhaps to their first baby. She was prone to daydreaming, to weaving romances about other people—but never about herself and couldn't think why. She wondered how she would take to life in the country after the rich brew of London. Would she find it too tame—too dull? Yet she had been born in the country and still had many ties there; her grandfather had seen to that. 'Life is what you make it,' had been one of his favourite sayings. That was all very well, but sometimes fate put its oar in, as she knew to her cost.

The train thudded into a station and jerked to a stop. Passengers bestirred themselves, pulling cases off the rack, and Laurie joined the half dozen or so leaving her compartment. As she stepped on to the platform her first impression was of colour. Flowers of all shades cascaded from hanging baskets on every lamp bracket and beyond the station buildings there were great beds of flowers on the embankment. After some of the seedy stations she had travelled through during her working days it was a revelation, and her heart was gladdened by the sight. The mist had rolled away, and now the sky sparkled. Beyond the station she could see the uplands rising into a hazy distance.

Outside the station was a cobbled yard where cars and taxis waited, and she could hear traffic not too far away. All about her was a quiet unhurried busyness, and she was the only one to stand there as if lost.

She had no idea what Dr Lawrence looked like, or his age, and she wished she had thought to ask Dr Russett, but in her excitement she had forgotten. It was turning hot. She untied the scarf from her throat and slipped it into one of the wide hip pockets—it was then that she saw him, a tallish slender man with hair so fair it gleamed like silver. Her heart leapt as if in recognition.

Years before when a student she had gone

with a party of other students for one never-to-be-forgotten week in Florence. Purposely she had never returned, for her stay there had been a near-perfect experience which she knew it was impossible to repeat. The impact of Florence on her, with its shimmering red-brown roofs, its massive palaces and works of art, the Baptistry—the 'Gates of Paradise', even the spring flowers filling the gardens with lingering odours—all that incredible beauty at an impressionable age had woven such a magic spell that she had considered herself in love. He had been a fellow student, one of their party—tall with coin-coloured hair; one of the other members had facetiously dubbed him David, after Michelangelo's statue, and the nickname had stuck because there was a certain likeness. The romance had not survived the journey home, but ever since then she had never been able to meet a tall blond man without that old feeling of elation flooding over her. It was the same now, and as she watched the fair stranger approaching her heart nearly stopped.

'You must be Miss Bush,' he said. 'I'm Nicholas Lawrence—I hope I haven't kept you waiting?' He held her hand a little longer than was necessary, smiling down at her with eyes just a shade darker than her own. 'You fit your description exactly—eyes as blue as the sky, hair the colour of night—and standing as high as a man's heart.'

She blushed furiously. 'I can't imagine Dr Russett saying that!'

'Oh, she didn't. She just gave me the basic details—I supplied the rest.' He hoisted her case from the pavement, his eyes flattering her all the time he was talking. 'This way—I had to park outside, there was no room in the yard.'

He stopped by a low brown-and-cream coloured sports car. 'Let me introduce you to Morgan, a present from an indulgent aunt. Do you mind travelling with the hood down? It's about four miles to Merton.'

He helped her into the passenger seat and put her case in the back. 'Thank you, Dr Lawrence,' she said shyly.

His left eyebrow shot up. 'What's all this Dr Lawrence? I'm Nick to my friends. What's your other name? Laurel! Were you named after a tree?'

She swallowed back her laughter. Her name—Laurel Bush—had caused her much teasing at school and she still got annoyed at some of the jokes at her expense, but nothing this handsome easygoing man could say would upset her, especially when uttered in such tones and with such a smile.

He was a good driver, negotiating the congested market place with care, but once away from the town and with a wide straight road ahead he put his foot down and the low-slung car thrummed along the metalled highway. Laurie imprisoned her flying hair with the scarf from her pocket, tying it securely under her chin. The wind had whipped more colour into her cheeks, and the countryside was scudding past so quickly she was unable to see anything in detail. She had an impression of stone walls and giant overhanging trees and every now and then a cluster of sandstone cottages or an old farmhouse, and always with them the rolling uplands in the colours of high summer where sometimes sheep and sometimes cattle grazed. Then on the horizon appeared the tower of a church, and her companion said:

'We're nearly there. That's the church of Merton-on-the-Hill—a landmark for miles.'

Merton considered itself a sizeable town, but to Laurie, fresh from London, it seemed just a large village. The church dominated a cobbled square with two other sides taken up by shops and hotels and large houses. Facing the church at the far end was a seventeenth-century market hall. Dr Lawrence went past this, then turned right along an unmade road marked Private. It led straight on to a wide open grassy space graced by a clutch of Scots pines in one corner. One side of the grassy square was occupied by a beautiful old stone house in expansive grounds, the other by a row of small cottages. Beyond was farmland.

Dr Lawrence parked outside the cottages. 'This road is private?' queried Laurie, easing herself out of the car.

38

'That's for the benefit of frustrated motorists who can't find anywhere else to park on market days. Joking apart, we do have to keep this part free for patients. The two end cottages comprise the practice, Shirley Dickson our dispenser occupies the other two—'

'Both of them?' exclaimed Laurie. There were two sets of semi-detached dwellings joined by an archway. There were two front doors to each set, a latticed window beside each door, and above, other windows set in steep gables. Sunlight picked out the stonework, turning it from dull grey to a warmer sand colour, and there was a riot of climbing roses growing across the length of the frontages. The whole was a chocolate-box scene of such charm that Laurie stood feasting her eyes on it, wondering that a chance ad in an evening paper should have made this all possible.

'Knocked into one now, and not as big as appears from outside. These were old almshouses, just one up and one down originally.' He flashed her a heart-stopping smile, then jerked his head in the direction of the arch. 'Shirley isn't in, otherwise the front door would be open. We'll go round the back, I know where she keeps the key.'

The arch opened on to green lawns and beds of late-flowering perennials, Michaelmas daisies and chrysanthemums. The two cottages on the right had a large modern extension which had swallowed up that part of the garden, the rest belonged to the other cottages; it wasn't large—it didn't need to be, for beyond was the rolling countryside.

'The key will be in the most obvious place, either under a flower-pot or the mat,' said Dr Lawrence, and almost at once retrieved it from under the milk-bottle frame. He opened the back door and they stepped into a small, low-ceilinged kitchen brightened by yellow paint-work and colourful pictorial tea-towels pinned up to every available wall-space.

The doctor carried her case through into the living-room and put it down. 'I'm sorry I'll have to dash off now, but I'm in the middle of my rounds. Shirley should be here any minute, I expect she's gone to the shops to get something for lunch. Why don't you make yourself a cup of tea while you wait—or better still, help yourself to a glass of sherry. I know where she keeps it.' It wasn't lost on Laurie that he was very familiar with Shirley's ways.

'Thank you, I can wait,' she said quickly, not wanting to detain him. 'I had a cup of coffee on the train.'

He shook hands again. 'Be seeing you.' His eyes glowed appreciatively. 'I'm glad you've joined the club!'

Laurie watched out of the window as he climbed into the sports car and then roared out of the close. She couldn't resist a little smile of gratification. Things were certainly looking up—her future seemed set fair.

She looked about her. She was in a double room, low and heavily beamed and divided in two by a massive central fireplace. Narrow spiral stairs curved up from one of the alcoves beside the fireplace, the other alcove had been opened up and rounded off to form an arch between what had once been two separate rooms. The floor was made of large slabs of stone covered with an assortment of rugs. There wasn't a lot of furniture—there was plenty of room for her own bits and pieces, she thought idly, then she quickly brought her thoughts under control. What was it Dr Russett had said on the phone? 'Shirley will be able to put you up until you find somewhere suitable to live.' So there was no use fostering hopes in that direction.

She could see why Shirley kept the door open in fine weather; there was very little light in the room. The windows were attractive with their twinkling diamond panes and deep triangular sills, but they were too small to be efficient. The second front door was obscured by a heavy curtain and then a television set in front of that; the room leading from the kitchen was obviously used as the dining area as a round mahogany table took up a lot of the floor space.

Suddenly the front door crashed open as if somebody had fallen against it, and a tall loose-limbed girl came bounding in. She had an

41

armful of shopping which she immediately dropped on to the table, her jacket she flung on the nearest chair, and this was followed by a paper and some books.

'So you're Laurie,' she said. She spoke with a slight North-Country accent. 'I feel I know you already, Dr Russett has been talking about you so much. Sorry to have kept you waiting, but there wasn't a thing in the house to eat after the holiday, so I've been along to the market place to stock up. Hope you don't mind just fruit and cheese, I haven't had time to cook anything.' She pulled a face. 'Not that I can cook anyway!'

'I didn't expect you to give me lunch,' said Laurie awkwardly.

'Good gracious, of course I must give you lunch! I had a three-course banquet waiting for me when I first started, but that was Pam's doing—Pam's the one you're replacing, in case Rusty forgot to tell you.' She pulled herself up, giggling a little. 'That wasn't meant with disrespect. Dr Russett is Rusty to everyone behind her back. Of course she knows, and I bet she wouldn't mind if we called her that to her face. I wouldn't like to risk her other nickname, though—the Big Apple.'

'The what?' queried Laurie, half laughing, half puzzled.

'The Big Apple—the other name for New York, y'know. And russet being an apple and Rusty not exactly sylph-like, the Big Apple

42

describes her down to the ground. Dr Ross thought that one up, and he's the only one who dares use it.'

Laurie could see she would have to revise her image of Dr Ross. White-haired, genial he might still be—but now he had an edge to his wit. Well, that only made him all the more human. Smiling, she helped Shirley carry her shopping through to the kitchen.

'Did Dr Lawrence show you the bathroom?' Shirley asked.

'No.'

'I thought not, but I bet he knew where to find the sherry. Anyway, go through the archway and it's the door at the end. It's the counterpart to this kitchen, actually; it was converted into a bathroom when the two cottages were knocked into one.'

The bathroom was far more modern than the one Laurie had left at Woodford, small but compact and furnished with a violet-coloured bathroom suite. She washed, and smoothed her hair, noticing how tidy everywhere was. The whole cottage was incredibly neat, so much so that she had guiltily picked up a piece of straw that had come in on her case. And yet the way Shirley had flung her things about! Within five minutes it looked as if a hurricane had hit the room.

Shirley had set up a picnic table under the willow tree on the lawn. 'We'll eat before I take you up to your room,' she said. 'I expect you're starving—I know I am. I always eat out of doors whenever possible,' she added. 'I like plenty of light, and that's one thing I'm short of in the cottage—otherwise it's perfect.'

It was perfect sitting out in the garden too, being serenaded by a robin and listening to the bees bumbling among the lavender. A feeling of contented drowsiness stole over Laurie; she had been up at six o'clock after a sleepness night—now the sun and the warm spicy air were together acting like a drug on her senses.

'Have another banana?' asked Shirley. 'No? Well, try some of these grapes, they're delicious. What did you think of Golden Boy?'

The question was so unexpected Laurie froze, her fingers still on the fruit.

'Golden Boy?' she echoed.

'Yes. Dr Lawrence has his nickname too.'

Shirley's voice was anything but flattering, and Laurie stole a look at her from beneath her lashes. She had what some artists call a mobile face, meaning expressive—but now it had a closed, secretive look as if she were hiding her thoughts. She was a strange girl, Laurie reflected; big, ungainly, untidy in her appearance. She was not unattractive, though her mouth and nose were large—but so were her eyes. They were her best feature and an unusual colour, more golden than hazel. Her hair, which was light brown, was cropped short above her ears, and did nothing to flatter her. It was as if knowing she had no feminine appeal she refused to pander to fashion.

'I can see you looking at me through those lashes. Well, will I pass?'

Laurie blushed. 'I'm sorry, I didn't mean to be rude. What did you mean about—well, Golden Boy?'

Shirley grinned. 'Do I detect a note of concern? How did he greet you? No, let me guess.' She stared hard at Laurie for a moment or two. 'I bet it was something to do with blue eyes and black hair, eh?'

Laurie's colour deepened. She had been treasuring the memory of those words—now they only made her feel foolish.

'Are you suggesting he's a philanderer?' she said stiffly.

'No, nothing as devious as that. Our Golden Boy just can't help flirting with every female he meets—regardless of age. He's always got an apt speech waiting for newcomers—especially the pretty ones; even for me. Though he was hard put to it to think up anything flattering to say to me!' She said it without rancour, laughing all the time. 'But I mustn't give you a wrong impression of our Dr Lawrence. He's a very good doctor and very popular—particularly with the ladies,' she couldn't resist adding.

'What about Dr Ross?' Laurie wanted to get off the subject of Dr Lawrence, she was feeling more uncomfortable every time his name was mentioned.

'Oh, Dr Ross is something else again.' And Shirley collected the dirty plates together and went into the kitchen to make coffee.

Afterwards she took Laurie up to see her room. It was small but exquisitely pretty, with wallpaper, curtains and matching duvet cover in a rosebud pattern. 'Oh, it reminds me of the bedroom I had when I was a small girl,' cried Laurie.

'There's not much room, I'm afraid, but your clothes will go in the space under the eaves. It makes a lovely closet, and there's the dressing-chest too—sorry there's no room for a bedside table.' Shirley opened the window and flung it wide. 'That's better, that lets more light in. Part of this room was chopped off to make into an airing cupboard, that's why it's so small.'

'It's quite big enough—after all, it's—' then Laurie stopped herself. She had been about to say, 'After all, it's only for one night,' but couldn't finish the sentence. She still nursed a secret hope. As if by telepathy Shirley turned and said very earnestly:

'I suppose you wouldn't consider staying here—sharing this cottage with me? No, of course not!—you'd rather have somewhere more modern or some place to yourself.'

'I'd love to live here,' said Laurie fervently. 'I've been dreaming of living here ever since I came—but are you sure? It's your home, do you want to take in a stranger?'

'We won't be strangers long, we'll be

working together,' said Shirley skittishly. She was like a schoolgirl in her excitement. 'Gosh, I'm pleased we've got that settled. Can you cook?'

'I haven't poisoned anyone yet.'

'Great! Pam was a super cook—we shared this place until she got married. Then I pigged it on my own for a time; then a temporary clerk at the practice moved in with me, but she didn't stay long either here or at the job. The clerk we have now lives at home still. Would you believe me if I told you I live on things on toast? Egg on toast, then beans on toast, then spaghetti on toast, tomatoes on toast—curried beans on toast, and so on ad infinitum, any permutation you can think of! Sometimes I get invited out, but not often. My reputation has gone before me—"Here comes that human vacuum cleaner," I can see my hostess whispering. "Hide the fruit flan and the trifle and don't let her help herself to the roast potatoes or there won't be any left!"'

Laurie's heart warmed to this large plain girl who could take the mickey out of herself with such relish. 'I don't believe a word you say,' she laughed. 'I bet you could cook if you wanted to. But I warn you, I'm not up to your standard of tidiness, so please have patience with me while I learn.'

Shirley stared. 'Are you pulling my leg?' she demanded. '*Me* tidy? What gave you that idea?'

'Everywhere was so neat—' Then Laurie

47

remembered thinking the living-room had looked as if a hurricane had hit it after Shirley had come in. 'You're not tidy?'

'Heaven forbid! No, I'm not tidy—what made you think I was? Oh, I know,' Shirley smiled. 'My Mrs Crisp came this morning—I'd forgotten, she usually comes on Wednesdays—sheer waste of time, but she insists and she doesn't charge much. Well, I'd better let you unpack. Rusty will be phoning through from the surgery soon. She's been waiting for Dr Ross to turn up. He travelled down from Scotland last night.'

Laurie had been wondering why she hadn't been summoned before this; her arrival seemed to be treated very casually, but she had decided things hadn't yet got back to routine after the holiday. She was just putting her empty case away in the closet under the eaves when she heard the phone ring, and shortly afterwards Shirley shouted up the stairs for her to come down.

'They're waiting to see you now,' she said. She had been washing up wearing a bright yellow plastic apron which stated in bold white lettering all over the front—'Don't shoot the cook, she was doing her best.' 'I'll just dash across the lawn with you and show you the back way in. I'm not supposed to leave the cottage unlocked. There was a break-in at the surgery a few months ago, nothing was taken, but since then Dr Ross has been very security-conscious.

He insists I lock up every time I go out, not that I bring any drugs home—but who's to know?' She showed Laurie through the back door and across the grass to the extension behind the other cottages. This was the waiting-room, dispensary and office, and was empty at present except for a girl clerk at one of the counters. She looked about seventeen and gave Laurie a smile. A corridor led through to the older part of the building and Shirley gave Laurie a push towards it.

'There you are—see you later, I'll be at the cottage. I won't be going out again, Tuesday is my afternoon off.'

Laurie wondered why she was left with such a feeling of apprehension. She had already been accepted by Dr Russett and Dr Lawrence besides Shirley, so why this sudden dread, this reluctance to meet Dr Ross? From what she had gathered she had nothing to fear from him. She screwed her handkerchief into a ball and dabbed at her face, which had begun to tingle all over: it always did when she was nervous. Then she saw Dr Russett coming along the corridor towards her and the very sight of her revived her confidence. There was something about Dr Russett which acted as a tonic for frayed nerves.

'Well, how are you, my dear?' she said. 'Come along, Dr Ross is waiting to meet you. You found your way all right? Good. I'm sorry I didn't come along to see you before, but I've been holding the fort on my own. We're having our first breathing-space since nine o'clock. Still, Shirley looked after you? Good. This way.'

She led the way through an open door to a room on the right, identical to one in the neighbouring cottages, but Laurie hardly realised this; her eyes were riveted on the man standing solidly in the middle, his head nearly touching the overhead beams, his slate grey eyes staring at her incredulously.

As her insides seemed to turn into water she heard his explosive, 'I don't believe this! This just couldn't happen!' She saw him take a grip on himself. When he spoke again the bluster was gone from his voice, but the icy politeness with which he spoke was more devastating. He said to Dr Russett:

'Do you know anything at all about this girl? I've met her twice before. Once at a perfectly straightforward nursing practical which she should have passed easily, but because she dropped some instrument or other she went completely to pieces and bodged the whole thing up. I met her again last Friday—on the Underground. She'd lost her head again—accusing some passing youth of stealing her wallet, simply on the grounds that she objected to his hair-style, I gathered—'

Laurie looked away, unable to meet the anger and contempt in his face any longer. She saw Dr Russett's expression of utter bewilderment and could almost have felt sympathy for her if her own feelings of anguish and despair had not blotted out all other emotions. Dr Ross's contemptuous tones broke in on her consciousness again, 'And there was her wallet in her basket all the time! Do you really think we can employ anybody so unstable?' He looked abruptly at Laurie again, shooting a question at her and catching her unawares.

'And when did you re-sit that practical? When did you finally qualify?'

CHAPTER THREE

This can't be real, Laurie was thinking. It's all a nightmare. I shall wake up in a minute and find myself back in the cottage or at Woodford with Sadie.

She realised that a question still hung, unanswered, in the air and that both Dr Ross and Dr Russett were looking at her. She braced herself for the inevitable reaction her answer would bring.

'No, I didn't qualify,' she said steadily. 'I didn't re-sit my practical.'

Dr Ross brought his open palm down on his desk with a vicious slam. 'You didn't qualify? You're not registered? Yet you had the impudence to apply for this post, knowing the terms—'

'Ross,' Dr Russett interrupted quietly, 'I think you and I had better discuss this matter further.'

He turned on her. 'Did she hoodwink you? Didn't you question her during the interview? You gave me the impression that you were well satisfied.'

'I am—and if you only would let me explain!'

'What is there to explain? The girl isn't qualified and that's an end to the matter.'

Laurie's self-control snapped at this point. All her pent-up fears and hopes suddenly came to a head and were released in a great burst of indignation—indignation that these two were discussing her as if she were not there—as if she were something devoid of sense and feeling. She turned her fury on Dr Russett first.

'If only you'd given me his correct name. Dr Ross—that meant nothing to me, but I wouldn't have come within five miles of this place to see a Dr Cramond!' Then to the staring man:

'As for you—the rest of the staff might look upon you as some feudal lord, but to me you're just an ill-natured, arrogant bore, and I wouldn't work for you for double the salary— no, not even if you trebled it! Do you think I'd belittle myself to the man who was responsible for me failing my finals in the first place? If it hadn't been for you I wouldn't be in the position I am now—I might have been a staff

52

nurse in a teaching hospital instead. And the way you spoke to me on the Underground! You're insufferable—I'd starve before I was beholden to you!' Then she turned and ran and the door slammed on the silence she left behind.

Still in her plastic apron, Shirley was sitting with her feet up on the table browsing through a week-old copy of the local paper when Laurie dashed past her and up the stairs. Shirley stared after her with her mouth open. After a while she stood up, took off her apron and climbed the stairs. She hesitated outside the spare bedroom door; she could hear Laurie crying.

She softly called her name.

The crying ceased. Then was a pause and then the door opened and Laurie looked out, her face wet with tears.

'What's happened?' asked Shirley anxiously.

'You may well ask!' Laurie opened the door wide and Shirley went in. She glanced at the crumpled bed where Laurie had thrown herself in a storm of tears.

'I'm not staying here, I'm leaving right now,' said Laurie wildly. 'Get me a taxi, Shirley, I don't care how long I have to wait at the station.'

'What's happened?' Shirley demanded again.

'I don't want to talk about it—I can't! Oh, Shirley, I'm so sorry it's turned out like this. I didn't mean to put you out—'

'You're the one who looks put out,' answered Shirley gruffly; others' distress always embarrassed her. There was a moment or two of silence while she stared at Laurie and Laurie stared wretchedly at the floor. Then came the sound of a door opening below, and a voice calling up the stairs:

'Shirley—Miss Bush, are you up there?'

'That's Rusty,' said Shirley, stirring herself.

Laurie came to life too, and hastily pushed Shirley out of the room. 'I don't want to see her, I don't want to see anyone. Say I'm packing—say I've already left—say anything, but tell them to leave me alone!'

It was a futile plea, for presently Laurie heard the tread of heavy footfalls on the stairs. She stood behind the bolted door clasping her hands together in an agitated way.

Dr Russett knocked. 'I want to speak to you, Miss Bush.' Then when there was no response, 'Laurel, open the door, don't be foolish. Don't you think we should be able to talk this thing over in a civilised manner?'

With an ill grace Laurie complied. Her eyes had begun to look puffy, and Dr Russett looked at her and shook her head. 'What a waste of good emotion,' she sighed. The bed creaked as she lowered herself on to it.

'Dr Ross agrees with me that we should take you on on a three-month probationary period, as I suggested in the first place. I hope you will

54

still agree to that, Laurel.'

Her manner was disarming, particularly the way she called Laurie by her full name. Only her grandfather had ever done that. But Laurie still found herself demurring.

'I'm catching the next train back to London.'

Dr Russett sighed, then patted the bed beside her. 'Come and sit here and let's talk.'

'There's nothing to talk about.'

'You want a job. We need a nurse. Don't you think that's a basis for discussion?'

Laurie looked away, out towards the small square of window that framed the large house across the Green. 'I thought everything had been settled on Saturday. I thought we'd done all the necessary talking then. Oh, why didn't you tell me his name was Cramond—why did you keep calling him Dr Ross?'

'Because that's the name he's known by, to distinguish him from his father in the first place—now it's a habit. You know, Laurel, I think he's truly sorry for upsetting you just now, though he wouldn't say as much. He asked me to ask you to stay. That, for Ross, amounts to an apology.'

'And how did you manage to twist his arm?' asked Laurie bitterly.

Dr Russett smiled. 'I reminded him that he has two auxiliary surgeries to visit this afternoon, and no nurse to accompany him if you left; I also told him to read your record as a student. He knows of the Beatrix Morse

Nursing Home, it has a good reputation among medical circles. All it comes down to is you taking your practical again, and you've already promised to do that, haven't you, Laurel?'

Laurie felt her resolution to leave on the next train ebbing away. She had nothing against Dr Russett, the more she saw of her the more she liked her, and she had struck up an instant rapport with Shirley. As for Dr Lawrence—but she mustn't think about Dr Lawrence, for her heart began to race in a disturbing way when she did. If it weren't for Dr Ross the situation would be perfect—but then Dr Ross *was* the practice, and one went with the other.

'How can I possibly stay after what I said to Dr Ross?' she sighed, thinking aloud.

'Well, you could go and apologise to him, but I don't think that would be a good idea. Ross is no better at accepting apologies than he is at making them. To be on the safe side I think you'd better confine your conversations with Dr Ross to professional matters in future, otherwise you two will be constantly rubbing each other up the wrong way. By the way, what did you mean by saying if it hadn't been for him you wouldn't have failed your practical?' added Dr Russett.

Not looking at the doctor, but resting her elbows on the deep windowsill and staring blindly out of the tiny window, Laurie recounted as briefly as possible the events of that fateful day. 'He expected me to fail,' she ended, 'so naturally I did fail.'

'And that was about two years ago—yes, the time his father died and he had to make the decision whether to return to this practice or not. You see, he always wanted to be a surgeon, so after a few years working here with his father he went off to London to specialise. He did very well, we were all very proud of him—then just when he was faced with most brilliant prospects his father died. He had a real tussle with his conscience then; he wanted to stay in surgery—but he knew it had always been his father's wish that he would carry on here.' Dr Russett's voice changed and she said, 'How odd, that mirrors your own difficulty—you had to face the same alternative; your duty or your personal wishes. Then you should have more sympathy for him, Laurel. Think what he was going through that day. Perhaps he was a bit hard on you—but he was being much harder on himself. Can't you forgive him?'

Laurie turned and stared bleakly at the other woman. She wanted to say, 'Why should I have to suffer because of his problems?' She wanted to cry out, 'What about me—think what I was going through too!' but she knew it would be no use. Dr Ross was something very special in Rusty's eyes—she would always be making excuses for him. And also, Laurie was a great believer in destiny, and so far destiny had plotted their lives in a most significant way.

Hadn't she herself said to Sadie, 'There are no such things as coincidences in my life'? This was more than a coincidence, it was something that was meant to be, so what was the point in trying to fight it?

'Yes, I'll stay,' she said finally. 'And I'll take my practical again—and pass! Dr Ross will never have another opportunity to throw up in my face that I'm not qualified.'

Dr Russett heaved herself off the bed and came to the window.

'See that house over there?' she said, pointing to the stone mansion opposite. 'Cramonds have lived there since they first came here from Scotland in the eighteenth century. Ross was born there. I know he's difficult to get on with—some would call him dour, perhaps a throwback to his Scottish ancestry.' She gave another sigh. 'I know I make allowances for him, perhaps because in different circumstances he might have been my son.' She didn't enlarge on this and Laurie was surprised at this sudden revelation. She hadn't been so wrong, then, thinking up a romance in Dr Russett's life. 'Things haven't been too easy for Ross in many ways,' the older woman continued. 'If you knew him as well as I do you would be more tolerant.'

'Does he live in that big house on his own?' asked Laurie.

'Not entirely. His father had three self-contained apartments made on each floor. I now share the ground floor with Ross's private consulting-rooms. He has the first floor, and the top flat was where the housekeeper and her husband lived until they retired last year. Now the flat is unoccupied and Mrs Crisp comes in and does for Ross, as they say.'

'I've heard of Mrs Crisp,' said Laurie.

'You'll be seeing a lot of her too. She cleans the practice as well as these cottages. Now, Laurel—and you don't mind me calling you by your first name?—we all do here; can you be ready in half an hour—to go with Dr Ross, I mean? Julie will find you a white coat.'

*   *   *

Laurie changed into a navy-blue denim skirt and a white blouse. The coat Julie brought across was several inches too long, but there was no time to deal with that then. In the half an hour's grace she had been given Laurie had taken a quick shower and given her hair a dry shampoo, and she felt ready now for anything; even facing Dr Ross again. All traces of tears had gone, but she looked pale. She pinched her cheeks—a little colour gave a sparkle to her eyes. She thought the white coat made her look like a pint of milk.

Dr Ross had brought his car over and it was parked outside the cottages, large with elegant lines—Laurie didn't recognise the make but thought it might be German. She hesitated on the pathway between the two lots of cottages, wondering whether to go back inside or wait in the surgery, then Dr Ross appeared, walking briskly and carrying two cases—his diagnostic bag and a dressings case which he handed to Laurie in silence.

He opened the near-side door. 'In here,' he said. There was no warmth in his voice; he was brisk, businesslike and impersonal. That's how it should be, thought Laurie, and wondered at her sudden surge of resentment.

He drove round the square, out into the main thoroughfare of Merton. They soon left the town behind, then plunged into deep, tree-locked lanes. He was not a fast driver, but he was competent and very sure. Laurie began to feel uncomfortable by the silence that gripped them like a clamp. She kept giving the man beside her furtive looks and couldn't help noticing how tired he looked. Well, he would, wouldn't he, she thought. Just back from the States on Friday, then a quick dash to Scotland and back for the weekend. It didn't even look as if he had had time to shave that morning because a shadow was developing around the line of his chin. Once he turned and caught her glance and she saw a gleam of grey eyes before he looked ahead again, and after that she kept her own eyes rigidly on the road in front.

Presently they were dipping down a narrow lane through a tunnel of beech trees towards a small hamlet straddled either side of a stream.

The only way across the stream was by a stone packbridge just wide enough to take a mule; two children hung from the parapet, a boy of about six and a girl somewhat younger.

Laurie wondered if this was journey's end until she saw the notice—FORD. Dr Ross slowed down and engaged bottom gear; effortlessly the big car slid forward into the water, and just as effortlessly climbed the incline the other side. The two children watched, both big-eyed, the girl with her thumb firmly locked in her mouth.

Dr Ross stopped the car, wound down his window and called across to them, 'How is your mother today?'

The boy grinned selfconsciously. 'She's fine, Doctor.'

'And how's your baby sister?'

The small girl took her thumb out of her mouth. 'She sleep a lot.'

'She don't at night,' her brother broke in. 'She yell then.'

'Do you want me to take her away again?'

The boy shook his head, still grinning, but the girl nodded solemnly, and Laurie saw what passed for a smile flicker across Dr Ross's face.

'Tell your mother I'll be along to see her later this week. I suppose you two young imps are waiting to see someone get stuck in the ford?' At that they both nodded rigorously. 'I thought as much—well, it's your father who has to come and tow them out. Take care then, and don't fall in yourselves.'

They drove on and out of the hamlet the other side. The trees gave way to drystone walling, and Laurie looked out over stripped harvest fields and saw pheasants pecking among the stubble.

'Do you drive?' asked Dr Ross suddenly, taking her unawares.

'Yes—I mean I used to, I haven't for about two years.' She saw no reason to tell him that she used to drive her grandfather about the quiet Suffolk roads in his old Rover. When he died she had got rid of the car. There was nowhere to garage it in Woodford, and in any case she lacked the confidence to drive in the London traffic.

'But you've kept up your licence?'

'Yes.'

There was another long pause and she thought the subject had been dropped, then he surprised her by saying, 'There's a small Fiat belonging to the practice which Shirley makes use of occasionally. Perhaps you'd like to do the same?'

She wondered if he meant for her own use, but he soon put her right on that. 'We keep it as a standby in case one of our own cars is ever out of action. You could use it if you're ever called out on your own—it does happen. You'll find things very different here from London,' he added. 'Our work isn't concentrated in one area, it's spread over many miles. My father could remember when country doctors visited their patients in horse and traps—some of the hardier ones even cycled. You might prefer to cycle.'

Was he mocking, or was this an example of his sense of humour? Laurie stole a look at him, but his face was impassive. 'I quite like cycling,' she said flippantly. 'It's good for the figure.'

She thought this would have been a cue for Dr Lawrence to pay her a compliment, but not Dr Ross, though he did give her a steady look that made her feel foolish. She knew that he knew she couldn't have cycled up some of these hills.

By now they were fast approaching another, much larger village. The river had widened out and ran parallel with the main street. There was a church and a post office and two or three shops. They drove straight through and out the other side, and stopped by the one-time station of a disused railway line.

Laurie was surprised to find this was the surgery, but her dismay soon vanished when she saw how well it had been adapted. The booking-hall was the waiting-room, and beyond, what had been the stationmaster's office and porters' room was now the doctor's surgery and the treatment room. About nine or ten patients were waiting, including a small boy who fixed Laurie with a blue-eyed stare as she walked past.

From now on it was purely routine work, and Laurie soon found her old expertise returning. There were injections to give, blood pressures to be taken, the nervous to be reassured and the old chronics to be comforted. The last patient was the small boy accompanied by his mother.

Laurie didn't take to the mother. She was a girl of about her own age, twenty-three, with thin dry hair dyed a dark magenta. Her face, naturally pale, was made to look paler by thick make-up and her lips were almost the same colour as her hair. She didn't look overly clean, her clothes were stained and her fingers discoloured by nicotine; by contrast the small boy looked robust. He had an aureole of reddish-gold hair and an impudent smile, and Laurie wondered how such an unattractive-looking woman could have given birth to such an attractive child. His right hand was bandaged.

'And what have you been doing to yourself?' asked Laurie as she was about to remove the bandage. She didn't miss the way the child gave his mother a quick sideways look before saying:

'I felled on the fire.'

'I'll see to Timmy, Nurse,' said Dr Ross abruptly, and shyly the small boy went to him. His mother looked away, staring out of the window. She seemed miles away, lost in thought.

Laurie saw with what gentleness Dr Ross

removed the bandage and the underlying dressing from the boy's hand, talking all the time in low tones, making sure that the young patient was more interested in what he was saying than in what he was doing.

'Yes, that's coming along nicely,' he said finally. 'Now go to Nurse and she'll put on a fresh dressing.'

Laurie was horrified when she had a good look at the boy's hand. She had seen enough accidents like this during her years at the hospital to realise this had only just escaped being a third-degree burn. 'What have you been doing to yourself?' she cried with concern.

Timmy leant forward as if he didn't want anyone else to hear. 'I felled—I told you, an' I put my hand on the fire.'

'You fell on the fire! A fire with no guard—and a fire in summer? Where was your mother when this happened?'

Both the girl and Dr Ross had turned at the sound of Laurie's angry voice.

'I was hanging out the washing, that's what I was doing,' said the mother, galvanised into life by Laurie's words. 'And you needn't look at me like that. I told him to stay in the garden with me, but it's like talking to a brick wall. I have to have eyes in the back of my head with him. If you think you can do any better, Miss Smarty, you try it—living in a damp cottage with no electricity and no bathroom—no nothing. No means of heating except for an open fire.

That's why I lit the fire—to dry the clothes and heat the water. But what would you know about that? I expect when you do your washing you just put it in the machine and push a flipping button. You don't know you're alive!'

The scathing words brought the colour to Laurie's cheeks. Now her own temper was aroused. 'Nobody with the right to call themselves a mother would leave an open fire without a guard in a house where there's a young child,' she retorted. 'It's just criminal negligence—'

'I think you'd better take Timmy to the treatment room,' said Dr Ross, interrupting her. He spoke quietly enough, but when she looked at him she could see he was shaking with anger. She realised then how badly she had behaved—how quickly she had forgotten one of the basic rules—never to criticise a patient in their hearing. Humbled, she took Timmy's other hand and led him to the next room. He looked up at her beneath his sandy-coloured lashes, a gleam of laughter in his eyes.

'Nurse Pam uster give me a sweetie,' he said hopefully.

'Oh, she did, did she? Well, I'll see what I can do if you stand quite still and let me put this dressing on.' In the next room she could hear voices in conversation—Dr Ross's cool and measured, the mother's becoming less agitated. 'And where did Nurse Pam keep the sweeties?' she asked, when the dressing was in

66

place.

'In that cupboard over there.' He rolled his eyes in the direction of the corner. The cupboard was locked, but Laurie had been supplied with a bunch of keys before leaving Merton and the third one she tried unlocked the door. There among the ledgers, the files and record books was a jar of boiled sweets. She let Timmy choose his favourite colour, and with his right cheek well extended he went off to join his mother again.

'Well, Timmy, I see you've had your reward for being a brave boy. Will you come and see me again next week?'

'Yeth, Doctor.'

Dr Ross looked at the mother. 'The hand is healing very nicely, Mrs Wilson. Bear in mind about not letting the dressing get wet, and I'll see you the same time next week.'

The girl nodded, her eyes downcast; she brushed past Laurie and out through the door, walking so quickly that Timmy had to trot to keep up. He turned and gave Laurie a cheeky wave. Out of the window Laurie could see him skipping along beside his mother—he was young enough still to live only for the moment and his moment was taken up with sucking a large lime-drop.

Laurie turned from the window to encounter Dr Ross's steely look. Her heart sank; just for a short time at the beginning of the sessions a tenuous rapport had sprung up between them.

Before patients a civility, if not warmth, had enlivened their manner towards each other, and once Laurie had even seen a look of admiration flash across his face as he saw her tackle a difficult injection. But all that was over now. He was the man she dreaded once more—the man of the examination room—the man on the Underground.

'Don't you ever do such a thing again,' he said in a voice as cold as charity. 'How dare you speak to a patient like that!'

'Timmy was the patient!'

'Will you please not interrupt when I'm speaking. You seem to forget that you are still very much on approval. Another outburst such as the one just now and you may as well take the next train back to London.' His voice softened just a trifle. 'If at any time you feel there's reason to criticise a patient come to me and have a word on the quiet—but never, *never* in front of the patient—and Mrs Wilson *is* my patient. I was treating her long before Timmy had his accident. Perhaps if you knew more about her you might have a little more compassion.'

Laurie's eyes blazed with fury. Compassion! What did this man know about compassion? She longed to say just that, but instead said:

'I still think she's an irresponsible person, and I hope the social services people are keeping an eye on her—'

'Damn you woman, will you stop making

snap judgments!' he bellowed in sudden passion. 'What have you against her—the colour of her hair? The same prejudice you showed towards that youth on the Underground?' He lowered his voice again, but still angry, added, 'That's the second time you've made me lose my temper today. What is it about you that has that effect on me? I don't usually lose control.'

She exchanged a cold glance for a cool one. 'At least it proves you're human.'

His face took on a grim smile. 'So you think I'm not human?'

She was about to retort that she didn't, but stopped, remembering his gentleness with Timmy, his concern for his other patients.

'You haven't shown much humanity towards me,' she said lamely.

Brusquely he answered, 'I think that says more for you than it does for me.' He gathered up his instruments and unused drugs and began to stow them away in their bags. 'We're both on probation, you and I,' he said after a pause. 'I haven't forgotten your threat to leave. As children say, shall we cry "pax"—just for the sake of the patients? Our ill-feeling towards each other may brush off on them, if not.'

If it was an olive-branch it was a very prickly one. Laurie gave a nod of agreement and went off to tidy the waiting-room. The only other words he spoke were to tell her there were two more calls to make and they were already running over their time.

They passed an old mill which had been converted into tea-rooms on the outskirts of the village. There were tables on the grass by the riverside and the sound of the weir came to them through the open car window. Laurie was longing for a cup of tea, her mouth had dried up with tension, but she knew it was useless suggesting they stopped. She felt that being told they were running late was in itself a rebuke, as if it were through a fault of her making.

Their way back to Merton was by another route and took them through a village called Lingwood. Here they stopped outside a small cottage, the middle one of three. A bunchy little old lady stood on the doorstep obviously awaiting them, nodding and smiling, eager to lead them in.

Laurie soon discovered that the front room of the cottage was rented as another auxiliary surgery, but that didn't interest her as much as the sight of the tea-things on a side table.

'Nobody waiting for me today, Mrs Hockin?' said Dr Ross, dropping his bags on to a vacant chair.

'Them that are well are going about their business, an' them that aren't are sleeping peacefully in the churchyard—except old Sam Bendip, an' he's just cantankerous,' replied Mrs Hockin complacently.

'What's the matter with old Sam?'

'His usual—the rheumaticks. I keep telling him to carry a potato about with him in his pocket, there ain't no better cure for the screws—but he won't have any of it; rather take them pills you give him.'

'Still trying to put me out of business, Mrs Hockin? Come on, how many other granny cures do you know of? I'm sure our new nurse here would be glad to learn from you.'

Mrs Hockin tittered, giving Dr Ross a familiar push. 'You do like you to have your little joke; you know I couldn't teach a young lady from London anything (Dear me, news travels fast in the country, thought Laurie) and I know you always laugh at my treatment for cramps.' She turned to Laurie. 'It's a sure cure—just sleep with a cork under your pillow. I always do; an old embrocation bottle cork, an' I never get cramp in the night now.'

'Ah, but it's very important the type of cork you use,' said Dr Ross, keeping a serious face. 'An embrocation bottle cork is the very thing—nothing finer, but I wouldn't have much faith in a champagne cork.'

'Get along with you,' said Mrs Hockin, giggling again. 'And where would I get a champagne cork? Now what about that cup of tea, Doctor?'

'After I've seen old Sam, but I think Miss Bush would welcome one.'

So he wasn't completely thoughtless. Laurie stood by the window and watched him cross the road to the cottage opposite. Mrs Hockin said, 'He's a lovely man—a real gentleman. I've known him man and boy—and his father before him. Now, my dear, come and try some of my Gloucester tarts.'

They were delicious, and so was the tea, served in eggshell-china cups. Laurie realised how keenly the old lady looked forward to surgery days, how she made the tarts specially and brought out her best service.

'You must give me the recipe for these,' she said, and couldn't have paid a higher compliment. Mrs Hockin put some of the tartlets in a bag for Laurie to take with her and also insisted she take some of the eggs from her free-range hens, and when it was time to go she picked a huge bunch of rudbeckias from the garden.

They were as large as saucers and their petals felt like velvet; brown and orange and gold. Laurie waited by the car with them in her arms while Dr Ross gave Mrs Hockin some last-minute instructions. She looked up and saw him towering there on the doorstep, dwarfing the little old lady at his side. He was smiling and talking amiably, and in his casual clothes—for he hadn't bothered to change out of the suit he had travelled in—and with that lock of hair which had again fallen across his forehead, he looked quite raffish. He caught Laurie staring at him and his eyes narrowed, gleaming; the look in them set her heart pounding. It was censure or criticism—but it couldn't be admiration—or could it? Perhaps it was the flowers he was looking at.

When he joined her he said, 'Just one more call, then back to Merton. You'll be pleased, it's been a long day for you.'

'Yes,' she agreed, wondering at this side of him that she had not given him credit for. Perhaps he was still under the influence of Mrs Hockin's gentleness—she hoped so, because she didn't want to cede him anything, even the ability to show consideration.

The next stop was the general practitioners' hospital on the outskirts of Merton. It was a pre-war building, in its own grounds, built of stone in keeping with the local architecture.

Dr Ross parked his car in the bay reserved for doctors. 'Would you rather stay here, or do you want to come in?' he asked.

Laurie's inclination was to stay—she was so tired every bone in her back ached, but she thought it would be more politic to show interest.

'I won't take long, I haven't any patients to see today, but I want a word with Matron.' He gave her a sardonic smile as they went through the swing doors. 'She's what you would call a Chief Nursing Officer, but out here in the sticks we tend to keep to the old nomenclature.'

Matron came forward to greet them, walking briskly with an air of efficiency about her. She was tall, well-built, with good eyes and a flawless complexion. Laurie, who had been expecting a younger version of dear Mrs Hockin, was caught off guard. The light-coloured eyes looked her up and down as they were introduced and the message in them was very plain: 'Hands off, he's all mine!'

Don't worry, you're welcome to him, thought Laurie as she watched them go off together to Matron's office. Both being so tall they made an imposing-looking couple. Marcia Peacock looked about the same age as Ross Cramond.

One of the nurses offered to take Laurie over the hospital. She was a chatterbox and soon informed Laurie that she had only left school eighteen months previously, that she was hoping to get to the County Hospital to train for her SRN and until there was an opening was working at the Cottage Hospital as a nursing auxiliary. Laurie was impressed by what she was shown. There were three wards, one each for men, women, and children; two treatment rooms, one equipped with a mobile X-ray machine, and four smaller rooms to isolate patients with infectious illnesses. All the rooms had been freshly decorated and there were flowers everywhere, and there was no sign of that haste or urgency that had been such a feature of the Eastside Hospital.

From a landing window she could look out over green acres of parkland where a flock of birds were grazing. She was puzzled, not recognising them. The young auxiliary laughed.

'They're young pheasants—perhaps you didn't know them without their tails. The farmer next door breeds them for the shoot and they're always coming over on to hospital land. Nobody minds; come October and there'll be pheasant on the menu, the farmer always sends several brace over with his compliments.'

'I think it's cruel, rearing birds just to shoot them for sport,' said Laurie hotly. 'They do it in Suffolk too, where I come from, but you wouldn't catch me eating pheasant.'

The girl laughed again. 'I don't see any harm in it—no different from eating chickens which have been reared for the same reason.' She was showing surprising discernment for one so young, Laurie thought. 'I could eat a plate of pheasant right now with all its trimmings—I'm starving! Come and see the kitchens—Cook's a darling, I can always scrounge something from her. Fancy a piece of fruit cake?'

From the corner of her eye Laurie noticed that Dr Ross and Matron were in the hall below, walking towards the door, Matron talking rapidly, gesticulating with her hands, and the man at her side nodding gravely. When they reached the door Matron put her hand on his arm as if to detain him a little longer. She seemed to be asking him something now, for he hesitated a bit, then shook his head, but at the same time smiling as if to take the sting out of his refusal. Nevertheless Matron looked disappointed.

'I'd better go,' said Laurie. 'Thank you for taking me over. I expect I shall see you again.'

'I hope so,' said the young girl blithely. 'I must go too or the others'll think I'm dodging bedpans.' She went off swinging her arms, bouncing as she walked. It didn't seem so very long ago when Laurie had been like that—so young, so eager—so full of assurance. And then that awful, fateful day of her practical when her world had disintegrated around her.

But she mustn't think any more about that; she had a chance now to start afresh; a chance even to forgive this man who had first shattered her life and was now the means of her rebuilding it. Could she ever forgive him? This morning she would have said no, but now she wasn't so sure. If he ever looked at her the way he was looking at Matron she might be put to the test, but there didn't seem much danger of that.

Then Matron said:

'Well, goodbye, Nurse, I hope you don't think too badly of our humble little hospital. We can't hope to compete with your London teaching hospitals or even fashionable West End nursing homes, but I still think we have an important part to play, don't you?'

Laurie had stammered something, she didn't know what, in reply; it wasn't until much later,

76

undressing for bed, that she thought of a suitable retort. It wasn't so much the words Matron had used as the sarcasm in her voice. She had intended to be offensive. And what made it worse was that Dr Ross had realised it and it had amused him, she had caught the gleam in his eye. Any softening of her resentment towards him had immediately hardened, and he had not said a word on the short drive back to the practice. He had not said much either when they parted; a word of appreciation would not have come amiss, Laurie told herself. Except for the minor calamity with Mrs Wilson she thought she had conducted herself successfully that afternoon, but she should have known by now that praise from a man like Ross Cramond was hard to come by.

Weary as she was, she didn't feel like sleep. She leaned on the windowsill looking out on to the quiet Green. There were no street lamps, just the moonlight, and by its beam she saw a man and a dog coming along the lane that led from the High Street. The dog trotted at heel, an extension of his master's shadow, and once the man reached down to stroke his head. Laurie drew back, hidden by the curtain, and watched as both turned into the house opposite and were lost in the shadows.

In a thoughtful mood she got into bed. Now why should that simple gesture of touching his dog make her think that Ross Cramond was a very lonely man? And what if he was!

It was not something she would lose any sleep over. She easily put him out of her mind and concentrated on Dr Lawrence instead, and she was still thinking of Nick Lawrence when she drifted effortlessly into sleep.

CHAPTER FOUR

Laurie slept heavily that night and was awakened into consciousness the following morning by a contrite Shirley.

'Sorry, Laurie—I did promise to call you, then I slept through the alarm. No time for coffee or toast, I'm afraid. Can you hang out until elevenses?'

'Of course.' Laurie was swiftly out of bed, fully awake. 'You're already dressed!'

'Yes, but I'll wait for you.'

It wasn't long afterwards that the girls walked across the garden to the surgery; but some patients had beaten them to it and were waiting. Shirley went off to the dispensary while Laurie joined Julie in Reception. Dr Russett wasn't long coming in. She left her handbag and cardigan in the office and slipped into a white coat. 'Come along with me,' she smiled at Laurie. 'Several TABs this morning— and already waiting, I see.'

It was a busy morning and Laurie was kept

on the trot until well after eleven o'clock, then she was free to make herself a much-needed cup of coffee.

The kitchen was the same size as the one in the other cottage but lacked the feminine touches. The back door stood wide open and sunlight streamed into the small cobbled yard. Two steps led down to an area of grass, all that remained of a one-time garden. Laurie took her steaming mug and sat down on the top step. The projecting wall of the annexe turned the yard into a sun-trap and as there were no windows on this side gave complete privacy.

'Any objection to me joining you?' Dr Lawrence stood over her, smiling down, the sun making a nimbus of his hair. 'I haven't seen you all morning. Have you been dodging me?'

'I've been in with Dr Russett.' Laurie edged up a bit as he sat down rather close. 'She's gone off on her rounds now. I don't know what I'm doing the rest of the morning.'

She couldn't trust herself to look at him, she was longing for him to suggest she paired up with him, but he said, with a touch of irony, she thought, 'I believe Ross wants you over at Sinclair House. He has two private patients to see this morning.'

He took a packet of cigarettes out of his jacket pocket and offered it to her, but she shook her head.

'Good for you! I wish I could kick the habit—I try every first of January, but by the

79

fifth I've given in. Don't look so disappointed, Little Tree, I'm not a packet-a-day man—more like a packet a week.'

At the ridiculous nickname he had given her Laurie began to laugh. He watched her, his eyes narrowed, then with a shrug put his cigarettes away again, unopened. 'If you flaunt your dimples at me much longer I shall kiss them,' he threatened.

Laurie didn't believe him, all the same she tried to straighten her face, but found it impossible—not with the way he was looking at her, with such a calculating, expectant expression.

'You asked for it,' he said. He carefully took her empty mug and put it to one side. Aware of his intention, she tried to jump to her feet—but was too late. He pinioned her with one arm and tilted her chin with his other hand. Then he kissed her, very tenderly on each cheek—but not at all tenderly on her mouth.

Breathless, Laurie pulled herself free, words of protest rising to his lips but inwardly thrilled by a sensation of pleasure.

There came a footfall behind them.

'Do you mind leaving that sort of thing until after surgery hours!' The command was crisp and coldly derisive.

Both jumped to their feet. The mug rolled away and down the steps. Laurie turned to face the accusing slate-grey eyes, but Nick Lawrence stepped in front of her and said,

'Hold on, Ross. It was only a bit of innocent play—'

'Do you mind playing in your own time in future and keep surgery hours for more important things!' The voice was scathing. The eyes that flashed from Nick back to Laurie showed his contempt. Nick looked annoyed but said nothing, and Laurie couldn't trust her voice. If it were to break it would be the ultimate humiliation. Ross swung on his heel and strode off, leaving an uncomfortable silence behind.

Beside her humiliation Laurie felt a sense of disappointment. Had Nick really meant the words he had given as an excuse—that it was only a bit of play? That would be a lot harder to bear than Dr Ross's scorn.

Then Nick caught her eye and grinned. He looked like a small boy who had been caught out, but eager to show his defiance. 'Don't look so down in the mouth,' he said. 'If you're going to get upset every time Ross barks at you, you're going to spend a lot of your time having the jitters! That's better—out come those bewitching dimples again! Don't worry, Laurie, I'll have a word with him and tell him it wasn't your fault—that I took you unawares—'

'No, you don't!' she cried hastily. 'I don't want you making excuses for me—not to him. In any case, you didn't take me unawares—' She stopped, realising the implication that could be put on her words, and he laughed.

'Right, I won't say anything, but you must let me try to make up somehow. How about coming out to dinner with me—you name the day?'

Laurie lowered her eyes in case her eagerness to accept the invitation was too plain. She said quietly, 'I'll see,' and after retrieving the mug slipped past him back to the kitchen. Shirley was there refilling the kettle.

'Dr Ross left a message for you. He wants you over at Sinclair House, it's the morning for his private work.' Shirley spoke over her shoulder. 'What's happened to make him look so mad?'

'He looked mad?' said Laurie innocently. 'I thought that was his usual expression.'

Shirley did not find this quip amusing. 'Don't play games with Dr Ross,' she warned, 'or you'll live to rue it!' but Laurie went out unconcerned.

It was with some reluctance that she crossed the Green to the house opposite. The deep baying of a large dog greeted her as she walked up the drive. She had always been nervous of dogs, and to her relief the barking stopped before she reached the house. The front door stood open, revealing a wide hall from which a mahogany staircase curved up to the next floor. There were a perplexing number of doors leading from the hall, but the one nearest to her on the right was helpfully lettered with the words Consulting Room.

Laurie tapped and went in. Ross was seated at a wide desk riffling through some papers. He gave her a quick glance.

'The office is through there,' he said, nodding towards an inner door. 'My first patient is a Miss Louise Fellowes. Would you bring me her file?'

The office, though small, was compact with everything to hand. Laurie found the file in a lovely old piece of furniture which had started life as a music cabinet. As she was shutting the drawer she heard the clip-clop of a horse's hooves on the gravel and looking out of the window saw a young woman just about to dismount from a well-groomed bay horse. Laurie didn't know much about horses, but she could recognise this as a splendid specimen. The girl walked the horse off to the stables, then reappeared, disappearing from Laurie's sight as she mounted the steps to the house. From the fleeting glimpse she had of her Laurie decided she was too thin for her height and she looked like someone living off her nerves.

The door between her office and Dr Ross's had been left ajar, and Laurie heard the girl enter the consulting room, then an exasperated sigh from the doctor.

'You're wearing breeches! You don't mean to say you rode a highly-strung horse like Cardinal through Merton on market day?'

'That's the very reason why,' came the quick

response. 'Have you ever tried driving down the High Street on a Wednesday?'

'You know very well I have—many times. And please put away that cigarette, I don't allow smoking in here. Nurse!' in a louder, more peremptory tone. 'Have you found that file I asked for?'

Laurie hurried through with the file, and put it on the desk. Louise Fellowes was lolling on a chair, her long legs in their well-polished boots thrust out in front of her. She would have been a very beautiful woman if she hadn't been so thin, but her thinness made her look very drawn and also made it difficult to assess her age, though Laurie thought she couldn't have been much older than herself. She smiled quite brightly when they were introduced, saying in a fluting, very light voice:

'Fancy you leaving London to work for an old grouch like Dr Ross!'

Laurie thought it best to make herself scarce, but Dr Ross called her back. 'Stay, Nurse, I want to give Miss Fellowes a thorough examination. Would you put the screen round the couch.'

The girl sat up sharply, looking annoyed, but he cut short something she was about to say with:

'It's no good glaring like that. I told you I'd have to give you a good check-up if you lost any more weight, and I don't have to get you on the scales to see that you *have* lost weight.'

84

'I'm not dressed for an examination.'

'I don't want you dressed—I want you undressed. Nurse will find you a gown. Please go and get ready.'

Later, when Laurie was in the office typing out the records from the rough draft of Dr Ross's handwritten notes, she could hear him and Miss Fellowes in conversation.

'You may think I'm harsh, Louise, but what I advise is for your own good.' She pricked up her ears. *Louise*. Was it more than a doctor/patient relationship? She read through the notes again and it was obvious in Dr Ross's mind that Miss Fellowes was suffering from anorexia nervosa. Laurie hadn't thought of that; the three or four cases she had nursed in hospital had all been of teenaged girls. She heard his tread on the floor and the sound of a door opening. He was seeing his patient out himself, not calling for her, Laurie, to do so. She went to the window and half hidden by the curtain watched. Louise Fellowes was tall, but Ross Cramond was taller still, by about four or five inches. He was looking down at her, talking gravely, and she was looking back at him with such worship in her eyes that Laurie felt an intruder and came away. She typed out the rest of the report with angry, jabbing fingers. The Matron of the Cottage Hospital and now Louise Fellowes—were there any more so blindly in love with Ross Cramond? She felt they needed their heads examining!

It seemed ironical that of the two private patients that afternoon one was suffering from near starvation and the other from obesity.

Mrs Coombe had all the complaints that stemmed from being overweight—flatulence, breathlessness, arthritis, indigestion and the risk of heart trouble. She also had a robust sense of humour and a hearty laugh.

'It's my heart this time, Doctor,' she said, easing herself into the chair Laurie had put ready for her. 'It feels as if it's come off its hook. Come to think of it, the hook feels as if it's slipped too!' She gave a bellow of laughter and Laurie wondered how Ross Cramond could keep such a straight face. He would have been joking with Mrs Hockin—why not Mrs Coombe?—or did money make a difference!

'And it will come off its hook if you don't lose that four stones I recommended,' he said, and Laurie realised then by the way his lips twitched that this was an old joke between them and the straighter he kept his face the funnier Mrs Coombe found it.

'Then you'd better have a word with my Hector, Doctor. He keeps bringing me back boxes of chocolates every time he goes to Birmingham. He's got a bit of a sweet tooth himself, and he has no patience with dieting. He says a little bit of what you fancy does you good—'

'The emphasis is on *little*, Mrs Coombe. All your trouble stems from being overweight—

your indigestion and arthritic pains could all disappear even if you could shed just two stones. Life would be easier for you too—you'd be more energetic, not tire so easily. Try a new diet.'

Mrs Coombe sighed. 'I can't resist food—I love it too much. I've always been a good cook and it's been a pleasure to cook for Hector, he's such a good trencherman. He doesn't like me cooking now—not since he made his money; he says we don't keep servants in order to work ourselves, so he keeps taking me out to dine instead. I tell you, Doctor, it's sometimes hard work trying to get through a five-course dinner, but I tell myself Hector has paid good money for it, so I'm not leaving any on my plate—not to be scraped off into the rubbish bin! Hector has worked hard all his life, so I'm not seeing his money go to waste like that.'

Laurie began to like Mrs Coombe, even if her logic was a shade unsound. She noticed what tiny feet and hands she had and guessed that she had been very slim in her young days as well as pretty. Dr Ross rose from his chair. 'I'll get you some more tablets for your indigestion and I'll give you a new diet sheet. This one isn't very drastic, so give it a try. Just think what a lift to your morale it would be if by the next time you come to see me you've several pounds lighter.'

Dr Ross was on the phone when it was time for Mrs Coombe to leave. Laurie walked with her to the door, and in that short while was given a potted history of her life. She learnt that Mrs Coombe had only lived in Merton for just over five years; that Mr Coombe had bought up the factory where he had started as a tea-boy fifty years before. That she thought Dr Ross was a charmer but awfully strict when it came to prescribing tablets. 'Do you know,' she stopped to face Laurie, her eyes enormous, 'I once asked him if he could give me some slimming tablets. He just *looked*—looked, my dear. I haven't dared ask him since. You don't know the way that man can look!' Laurie smiled rather humourlessly. 'I know I eat too much, but I can't help it.' A deep sigh. 'I find I eat when I'm lonely; don't you think that's a strange thing, Nurse? There I am in that big house with nobody to talk to and Hector miles away in Birmingham most of the time, so what do I do—I nibble. Chocolates, biscuits, nuts— it's not because I'm hungry, it's because I'm bored. Oh, I don't want you to get the wrong idea,' as Laurie's expression changed. 'I love Merton, I really do—the lovely countryside an' all—it's just that I haven't any friends here— real friends, I mean; like I had in Birmingham, where we were always popping into each other's houses for tea or coffee.' She suddenly began rummaging into her capacious handbag. 'Here's my card, dear, Hector had them printed when we first moved here, but I've hardly used any of them.' She gave a selfconscious giggle. 'It looks posh, doesn't it? I hardly recognised myself—Mrs Margery Coombe—everybody called me Midge at home—I mean in Birmingham. Anyway, dear, what I was going to say is, any time you have an afternoon off and don't know what to do with yourself, just come and see me. I'd really like that, and you don't have to phone first.'

Laurie watched her drive away in the sort of car that only a wealthy, indulgent husband could afford with very mixed feelings. The poor woman needed help, she was desperately lonely—diet sheets were no earthly good, couldn't Dr Ross see that? She was angry with herself for the sudden sense of disappointment that went over her.

He looked at her as she entered the room. 'Mrs Coombe seemed to have a lot to say for herself.' So he had been watching them out of the window.

She had meant to go straight through and back to her typing. What was it that stopped her, made her lean on the desk with her hands and stare at him defiantly? Surely some innate wish for self-destruction, she decided later.

'Do you know what's wrong with Mrs Coombe?' she demanded. 'She's bored out of her skull! She's got too much money and too much time and not enough to do. Her husband indulges her—won't let her do anything for herself—says that's what he pays servants for. He says she's worked hard enough in the past, now that she has the chance she must sit back and take it easy. Take it easy! Doesn't he realise that he's slowly killing her? She hasn't any children, that means no grandchildren to make things for or to visit her. She's lonely— she hasn't anybody to talk to. She feels out of her depth with her neighbours; one's a retired Brigadier and the other two are a business couple always jetting about the world—to use her own words. If she had something to occupy her, something to make her feel useful, she wouldn't feel so lonely, and it's because she's lonely that she's always cramming goodies down her throat. She's using food as a comfort, don't you see that, and all you do is offer diet sheets as a palliative!'

He was silent for a long time, looking at her steadily with narrowed eyes. Laurie saw a pulse throbbing in his neck and could only guess at the silent anger that gripped him. She was suddenly overwhelmed with horror at her presumption and felt the colour drain out of her cheeks. She couldn't hold his gaze any longer. She stepped back, looking miserably at her hands.

'Congratulations, Nurse,' he said sneeringly. 'You managed to get more information out of Mrs Coombe in ten minutes than I've been able to in three visits. Now if you'll be so kind as to get these letters typed for me this afternoon and leave them for me to sign, I have some calls to make now, and you'd better return to the practice.'

It was a civil but curt dismissal—she wondered if for good. She had certainly overstepped the mark this time. 'Oh, you idiot—you idiot!' she chided herself angrily as she crossed the Green. She couldn't keep the tears back. Such a short time ago Nick Lawrence had kissed her—now she was likely to be sent away and would never see him again. She hurried into the staff cloakroom and splashed cold water into her eyes. Coming out, she bumped into Shirley.

'Rusty's looking for you—she's got a distraught mother, a toddler who's swallowed a ha'penny and a baby with colic—all the same family. Good luck!'

'Where's Dr Lawrence?'

'On his rounds. Why?'

'No reason.' Laurie headed for Dr Russett's room. She expected any minute to get her marching orders and was hoping to see Nick Lawrence one more time, but as the morning wore away and no summons came her spirits slowly began to rise again. At twelve-thirty when Dr Russett said, 'Emergencies only now, no more appointments until three o'clock. You can pop off and get your lunch if you like, Laurel,' she felt a sense of reprieve. Or was Dr Ross waiting until he came back from seeing his own patients before giving her her marching orders?

Shirley was still in the dispensary with three

or four patients waiting for tablets. Laurie made signs that she was going across to the cottage, and by the time Shirley joined her she had made omelettes out of the eggs Mrs Hockin had given her the day before.

'This is something like,' said Shirley with relish. They were eating alfresco again, under the willow tree, with plates balanced on their laps.

'Well, it was my turn to get a meal. You had a lovely supper waiting for me yesterday.'

'Big deal! All I had to do was keep it warm— Chinese takeaway. I'm glad you liked it.'

'I enjoyed every mouthful, I was starving.'

'You looked too tired to talk last night, but I've been dying to ask you. How did you get on yesterday—with Dr Ross?'

Laurie chewed slowly, gazing abstractedly before her. 'All right, I think—but I also think that will be the first and last time I'll be visiting the auxiliary surgeries with him.'

'Oh? Why?'

'Because I made a fool of myself this morning, talking out of turn as usual. Oh, Shirley, I don't know what it is about that man—but whatever I mean to say to him always comes out differently. I know I'm in for the chop now—I really went over the top,' sighed Laurie.

Shirley didn't look any too concerned over this news. 'I shouldn't worry,' she said. 'Dr Russett has a very high opinion of you and Dr

Lawrence is looking forward to having you with him when it's his turn to do branch surgeries tomorrow.'

'You mean there's others!'

'Just two more—and you must know by now that Dr Lawrence always gets his way.' There was a knowing look in Shirley's eyes as she said this, and Laurie wondered if she too had witnessed the little drama played out in the yard that morning.

By mid-afternoon, when nothing had been said about her impudence to Dr Ross—for by now she was admitting to herself that that was what it was—she began to breathe freely again. Routine work had slackened off and she was free to go over to Sinclair House to type out the letters for Dr Ross. She had finished and was just tidying her desk when Dr Russett surprised her.

'Ah, Laurel, you're free—that's good. I've just come over to make myself a cup of tea and was hoping you could join me. I want a little chat with you.'

With leaden heart Laurie followed her across the hall, knowing in her bones what the chat was going to be about. Just when she thought she was out of the wood, too!

Dr Russett's flat was much bigger than Laurie had expected, remembering the flat she had shared with Sadie. This was three times the size with large square rooms. Dr Russett took her into the kitchen and plugged in the kettle.

'I hear you've had a disagreement with Dr Ross over two of his patients,' she said quietly.

Two? Laurie thought hard, then remembered Mrs Wilson. That seemed a long time ago now.

'I did speak out of turn, and I'm sorry. But I don't suppose he'll accept my apology.' It cost Laurie a lot to say that.

'I don't think Ross is interested in apologies, more in getting the facts straight.' Dr Russett made the tea and brought the tray over to the table. 'You must give him more credit for common sense, you know. He knows very well what Mrs Coombe's problem is, but he has to be very careful in the way he deals with it. It's a delicate subject—especially where Mr Coombe is concerned. No man who has spent so much money in providing his wife with every luxury wants to be told she's eating her heart out from loneliness. As a matter of fact Ross had already asked me to have a word with Mrs Coombe. Not in my professional capacity—I don't have private patients, but just a little heart-to-heart as one woman to another. He thinks my experience in psychology might help.'

'Both his private patients are in need of psychology,' said Laurie without thinking.

Dr Russett gave her an appraising look. 'You're very perceptive, no wonder Ross was impressed by you.'

'*Impressed*!' Laurie couldn't believe her ears.

'Yes, impressed—but not too pleased. Don't

94

goad him too far, he can be very frightening when he's really aroused.'

They drank their tea in silence. Presently Laurie said:

'Did he tell you the whole story of my little difference of opinion with Mrs Wilson yesterday?'

'He didn't go into details, so I'd like to know what really happened.'

Dr Russett listened thoughtfully as Laurie related the circumstances, then she shook her head. 'You know, you're being far too hard on Lucy Wilson. She hasn't any friends—purely her own fault, she's what your generation call a loner. Nobody knows her history, not even if she's really married—but one thing we do know, that she's extremely fond of her little boy.'

Laurie looked sceptical. 'Not fond enough to keep an eye on him, and he looked as if he hadn't had a bath in days!'

'But he looked well-nourished, didn't he? Poor Lucy exists on State hand-outs, and it's not our place to comment if she decides to spend most of it on food rather than on soap—'

'And a good proportion on cigarettes,' put in Laurie, remembering the nicotined-stained fingers.

Dr Russett gave a wry smile. 'I see the case against Lucy Wilson is proved as far as you're concerned. Perhaps we'd better give her a rest now. What about coming to see the rest of my pad?'

There was only the one bedroom, enormous with an ensuite bathroom, then a living-room and a slightly smaller study. There was still one room yet to be viewed, but Dr Russett hesitated at the door and Laurie wondered if she thought it too untidy to be shown off—but she couldn't have been more wrong. When at last the door was flung open with a theatrical flourish, Laurie let out a long gasp, exclaiming, 'Gracious, what a lovely room!'

The walls were covered in the palest pink silk delicately patterned with scenes of birds and flowers, and the same Chinese motif was continued in the pink and white carpet and the vases on the antique drum table and oyster inlaid cabinet. The two sofas and easy chairs were upholstered in a deep rose-coloured damask, matching the same shade as the velvet curtains that hung at the ceiling-to-wall windows. A gilt chandelier hanging from the centre of the ornate ceiling and the heavy gilt frame which encircled the looking-glass over the high marble mantelpiece added to the impression of eighteenth-century opulence.

It was indeed a beautiful room, but not one Laurie felt she could live with. She would have been frightened of sitting on the dainty gilt chairs or disturbing the many satin cushions on the sofas. She preferred the other rooms with their good but well-used furniture, but she couldn't hurt Dr Russett's feelings by suggesting so. She said noncommittally, 'I've never seen anything so sumptuous before.'

'Outside a museum or a stately home, you mean?' Dr Russett met her eye with a somewhat satirical look. 'It's not my room—I'm just its custodian. One of the conditions when I first leased this flat from Dr Cramond was that I'd leave this room just as it is. It belonged to his wife—her own private drawing-room—I think she sat in it at least twice!' Her voice was definitely censorious, now, and Laurie was startled by it. 'He had it redecorated for her when Ross was a baby—just as she wanted it—just like one she'd seen in a book. No expense was spared—it must have cost a fortune, but she was never comfortable in it—who would be?—and later, after she'd gone, it was just kept as a memorial.'

'She died?'

Dr Russett gave Laurie an odd look.

'You may as well know the full story now,' she said. 'You'll hear soon enough—different garbled versions from various sources, and I think I owe it to Ross to let you know his background. You might have a different impression of him then.'

She led the way back to her study. There was an old-fashioned chesterfield facing the garden and the door was open. Their view was almost that in itself was worth feasting the eyes upon.

Dr Russett seated herself and motioned Laurie to sit beside her. As soon as she began to speak, Laurie found herself absorbed in the history of a small boy born to a mother only eighteen years old and a father nearly forty— the loving awe he had always felt for his father, but the near-worship of the fun-loving girl who was his mother.

Then came the day when she just disappeared from their lives. He was five years old, too young to be told she had run away— and why; easier all round, especially for Dr Cramond's pride, to let him believe she had died.

'It was another man, of course, someone nearer her own age,' said Dr Russett sadly. 'I can forgive her for falling in love, even for leaving her husband—but never for forsaking a small boy whose whole life revolved round her. He got over his loss in time, small children do, but he never forgot her. He would talk about her endlessly, mostly to me—he soon learnt that the very mention of her name brought such a look of pain to his father's face. Then from the age of fourteen he never mentioned her again, and I found out he had discovered the truth—either from a servant or someone at school. He changed overnight from a happy-go-lucky, outward-looking boy to a quiet, morose, even sullen man; yes, he grew up fast. From that time on he mistrusted all women, was never comfortable in their presence—with the exception of those under ten and over sixty,' she added, with one of her wry smiles.

'It's a long time to bear a grudge,' said Laurie thoughtfully.

'He was betrayed at a very vulnerable age— also he could see what his mother's treachery had done to his father. He never forgave her for that. I'll always believe that it was to make up for the day she'd let his father down that he sacrificed his ambition to be a surgeon to carry on the practice here—making atonement, if you like.' Dr Russett pulled herself off the settee. 'Well, no more nattering—I've got evening surgery tonight. First I would like you to deal with some correspondence for me. Could you come over when you've finished here, Laurel?'

Laurie had already tidied both desks in the consulting-rooms. She put the cover on her typewriter, locked both doors, then went out, shutting the main door of Sinclair House behind her. She stood for a while on the top step looking over the sweeping drive and towards the Green. In a nearby clump of trees rooks were fussing around the deserted nests. She stood musing, thinking over what Dr Russett had told her. She could feel sorry for Ross Cramond as a small boy, but the man still aroused feelings of hostility in her. Besides, she remembered too well the way the Matron of the Cottage Hospital had fawned on him and how Louise Fellowes had adored him with her eyes. She couldn't believe that he was indifferent to such overt admiration, and she decided that Dr Russett had over-dramatised her story.

CHAPTER FIVE

The last two weeks of August and the first week of September turned unseasonably cold and with almost continuous rain, then in the usual English manner the weather suddenly reverted to sunny days as warm as in high summer. By mid-September when touches of autumn were showing in the turn of the leaves Laurie was so well established in Merton that her old life of rushed journeys and crowded tubes seemed like a not-too-happy dream.

The sweetest thing about her new life was her growing attachment to Nick Lawrence. He was the last to fill her mind at night, the first to recall the next morning; the days she didn't see him were days wasted, in her opinion—and the happiest days of all were the ones she spent out at the other two auxiliary surgeries with him.

They were held in two adjoining villages, one really a hamlet of the other—Upper and Lower Wingfield. At Upper Wingfield, the hamlet perched on a hill, the surgery was held in a large caravan, but not large enough to hold more than four or five people comfortably at any one time—luckily there were never more than that; they were a healthy lot in the Wingfields. Lower Wingfield was much larger and the surgery was held in the village hall. The caretaker, a crabby old man, got it ready for them and took it upon himself to act as receptionist and give a running commentary on everyone he saw approaching.

''Ere comes Mrs Mayes about her bunions— I can tell that be the way she's walking. That's what comes of buying shoes at jumble sales—as if she couldn't afford to buy new ones! Found the money to go to Benidorm two years running, didn't she?' 'An 'ere's old James Skepton—nothing wrong with him but bartender's elbow, he should try staying home and watching telly for a change.' 'An' would you believe it—'ere's that Maggie Yare. What she come for? Nothing wrong with her last night when they held Bingo here; last one to leave— yap-yap-yap—I couldn't get her out of the place. It's a different story this morning, a face as long as a bus; 'spect she's had her rates bill— that allus socks them.'

'Do you think this is ethical?' Laurie whispered to Nick the first time.

'No, it isn't, but it's vastly entertaining,' he grinned back.

Afterwards old Ned made them tea—a far cry from Mrs Hockin; no eggshell china or homemade cakes, Ned's tea came stew-coloured and served in mugs, but to Laurie, sitting on the back step of the village hall drinking it with Nick, it could have been nectar.

One of the happiest occasions to look back upon was a brief visit from Sadie and John at the beginning of September. They were having a belated honeymoon touring the Cotswolds, and booked in at an old coaching inn in the market square at Merton for two nights. One evening after the first warm sunny day for weeks they all sat out in the cottage garden drinking coffee and liqueurs and talking. Shirley and John soon got into a discussion about the different methods of marketing drugs, which gave Laurie and Sadie a chance for a private chat.

Sadie had just made Laurie promise to stay with them if she ever came to London, then looking about her she added, 'Not that I expect you'll ever want to leave this peaceful spot.' She gave Laurie a speculative look. 'Do you remember how I had to push you into applying for this job—any regrets?'

Laurie shook her head, thinking of Nick. 'None,' she said, smiling complacently.

While at Merton Sadie had made arrangements with Laurie for the dispatch of her furniture, and it arrived the following week. 'Very nice,' said Shirley, looking around when the last piece was in place. 'It gives a certain tone to this room. Am I allowed to sit on that chair?'

'Not on your life! That's for looking at only.'

Laurie had experimented with her bedroom, changing the furniture around, trying to squeeze out an inch or two more floor space. Finally she put the bed under the window and the chest of drawers against the opposite wall—this at least gave her easier access to the eaves cupboard. She was no longer able to stand at the window looking out, which she had liked doing, but now she could lie in bed and see the tree-tops and watch the rooks streaming across the sky. Last thing every night when she was in bed and usually reading she would hear footfalls on the path that bordered the Green and knew it was Ross Cramond returning from his nightly stroll, with Fergus trailing him like a shadow. In spite of the fact that she still felt only hostility towards him she couldn't help hoping that Dr Russett would invite him in for a nightcap. It was a large house to be lonely in.

And today was going to be another scorcher—even though October was nearly on the horizon. Under her white coat Laurie was wearing a new pale blue cotton dress, telling herself that if she didn't wear it now it would be out of date by next summer. It was Shirley's free afternoon and she was spending part of it at the dentist. Laurie had sympathised, but Shirley didn't seem all that concerned; she even put on a clean blouse for the occasion.

It was lunch-time, there were no more

103

appointments until two-thirty and the surgery was unusually quiet. Julie had gone home for lunch, Dr Russett was still in her office, Nick Lawrence was out visiting, and Dr Ross— Laurie didn't know where Dr Ross was and she didn't much care; she was eating a sandwich in Reception, having promised Julie she would attend to any phone calls.

When the phone did suddenly shrill she jumped, it made such a clatter in the quiet. She picked it up. 'Merton Surgery.'

'Oh, is that you, Nurse, I thought I recognised your voice.' Laurie recognised the caller too, a Mrs Lomax of Lynch Green—the village where Timmy Wilson also lived—a pleasant, busy little person with a trying old father. 'It's me father again, Nurse, he's wheezing something awful and he's only just told me he needs a new inhaler—the other's run out.'

'Do you want a doctor to come out to see your father?'

'No—no, Nurse, don't worry the doctors, my father can manage fine if he has his inhaler. I'd come and collect a new one meself, but there isn't a bus till four o'clock and that'll make me too late back to get his supper. He gets very crotchety if his meals aren't on time.'

'Don't worry, Mrs Lomax, we'll get a fresh inhaler out to you as soon as possible,' Laurie assured her. 'In the meantime should he get worse have you anything else you can use to ease your father's congestion?'

'I've got some menthol crystals, Nurse, they're marvellous for clearing the chest—just a few in some hot water. It's just getting Dad to have a good sniff, he can be so stubborn at times.'

Laurie hung up and went to tell Dr Russett the problem.

'I could take the inhaler out to Mrs Lomax,' she offered. 'I could be there and back before you start your clinic at two-thirty.'

Dr Russett smiled at her. 'How do you feel about driving on your own?'

'That's no problem—after all the help I've had from you and Shirley and Dr Lawrence I should think I could apply for my Advanced Driving Test!'

'I wouldn't be too sure of that.' Dr Russett glanced at her watch. 'Julie will be back soon—I can answer the phone if it rings. Yes, you go off, Laurel. I'd like you back here as soon as possible, but for goodness' sake don't take any risks.'

Ten minutes later Laurie was crossing the Green to Sinclair House where the Fiat was garaged with the other cars in the old stable block. She had loosened her hair and slung a lightweight cardigan over her shoulders, the inhaler was in her shoulder bag and she was wearing high-heeled blue sandals. They were made of kid and had come from Italy and cost a lot more than she could afford. They weren't suitable for driving, but she eased her conscience by telling herself that precious time would have been wasted looking out another pair of shoes.

As she walked across the cobbled stable-yard (not easy in high heels) she saw Ross Cramond's BMW parked next to Dr Russett's Fiesta; so he wasn't out as she had hoped. Though since those first ill-fated days at Merton her relationship with Dr Ross had been most correct—respectful on her part, distant but courteous on his—she could not dispel the feeling that a kind of time-bomb was ticking away between them. Even the sight of his car was enough to make her heart lurch with apprehension. It lurched even more at the sound of a deep-throated snarl as Fergus the golden Labrador leapt out of the shadows and crouching low on his belly confronted her with baleful yellow eyes.

With pounding heart Laurie stood her place. No good telling herself that everybody else thought the dog a gentle-hearted old softie; that Shirley worshipped him and often took him for walks; that she had once seen a child hanging round his neck—that didn't ease the fear and distrust she had of him.

'Go away—go away, you brute!' she snapped, flapping her bag at him ineffectually.

He brought his lips up in the way that terrified her, showing his teeth. She always thought of him as 'Fergus the Teeth', and it wasn't meant as a compliment.

'I hate you, you ugly brute!' she told him with sudden vehemence. 'I wish you'd go and get lost!'

'That would solve so many of your problems, wouldn't it, Miss Bush?' said a sardonic voice behind her. 'I daresay you would like to see me get lost too—wouldn't that be convenient?'

She had to force herself to turn and face Dr Ross. He was also showing his teeth in a somewhat frosty smile; she felt in a no-man's-land of panic between an outraged master and his vicious pet.

'Fergus won't harm you,' he said in an offhand way. 'It's just his way of showing his contempt.' (You're both good at that, Laurie thought.) 'Dogs can smell fear and take advantage of it—show him you're not frightened of him. Order him away and mean it; he'll obey.'

She wasn't sure if that was a command or a statement, she licked her dry lips and Dr Ross cleared up her doubt by saying peremptorily, 'Go along, then!'

She looked at Fergus. He still crouched low—still eyed her menacingly. She licked her lips again, cleared her throat and tried to shout, 'Out of my way—down—get back!' but none of these words came out—just a little whimper as her voice broke.

Ross gave her a look of cool derision, then barked a sharp command to the dog. Fergus

107

immediately padded over to him, sat at his feet and stared blankly away as if he had no connection with the present company.

'That's the way to do it.' Dr Ross put his hands in his trouser pockets and began to rock backwards and forwards on his heels, enjoying Laurie's discomfiture. 'What are you doing here, anyway?'

Laurie explained as curtly as possible about Mrs Lomax and the inhaler for her father.

'I see.' He was thoughtful for a moment or two. 'Do you know your way there?'

'I should do—I've been enough times.'

'Yes, but not on your own. You'll have to negotiate the ford at Yaxley—do you think you could manage that?'

She resented the tone of his voice and the assumption that she was an inept driver. She jutted her chin and said pertly, 'I know all about fords.'

'Good luck, then.'

She hoped he would go back into the house, but he stood in the drive watching her back out of the stable yard, and of course she clashed the gears. Her nervousness mounted as she proceeded down the drive in a series of jerks—running on kangaroo petrol, Shirley would have called it. Through the rear window she saw Dr Ross looking after her, his expression a strange mixture of amusement and scorn. But once she was away from the Green and cruising down the High Street her nervousness left her and soon she had left the narrow lanes of Merton behind and was out in open country.

She had only lived in the Cotswolds a matter of weeks, but already their magic had taken such a hold of her that Shirley was constantly teasing her about it.

'You think these are hills—you should see the fells of my Cumbria, they make these look like ramps! Still, I grant you there is a charm about this place. I love it too.'

Laurie was beginning to enjoy this little drive out on her own; the way was familiar to her by now and she encountered no snags until she coasted down the hill towards the hamlet of Yaxley and the ford, and realised that the river was in full spate. The gentle tumbling stream had doubled in volume and the water was gushing in a miniature waterfall under the bridge.

She had one moment of panic, then she put her foot down hard on the accelerator—the best thing, surely, was to get through it as quickly as possible. She realised her mistake when the car stalled in midstream, the engine spluttered and died—and there she was marooned, with the river surging around her.

She looked hopefully towards the bridge, but the Lovelock children weren't there—no, they'd be at school. She looked towards the farmhouse, its roof just visible above the surrounding trees, but there was no signs of life there either; Mrs Lovelock would be feeding the baby. There was nobody about, not even a dog to bark at her and attract attention. Laurie began to shout and to sound the hooter, but she knew it was pointless, there was nobody to hear her; that only left one alternative—she'd have to get out and wade.

First she took off her sandals. She had lost her dignity, and she was going to ruin her dress—no point in spoiling her new shoes too, she might as well salvage something from the débâcle. She slipped them off, placed them on the passenger seat with her bag, hitched her dress up to her waist and stepped out.

The water was cold, she hadn't expected that, and she gasped involuntarily, but fortunately it only came up to her waist, and she was coping quite well until she tripped over a large slab of submerged stone and fell headlong. She came up gasping and spluttering, water streaming from her hair and her face—two more faltering steps and she was safe on the roadway—safe but extremely wet.

When Mrs Lovelock with her baby in her arms opened her front door and saw Laurie standing there drenched to the skin and dripping all over her doorstep, she didn't have to be told what had happened.

'I'm sorry to knock you up like this,' said Laurie through chattering teeth, 'but could I use your phone?'

'Not until you've come into the kitchen and dried yourself down—you'll catch your death standing there! Come you in—this way—'

It was a real old-fashioned farmhouse kitchen with a coal-fired Aga. Laurie stood by it and rubbed herself all over with the warm towel Mrs Lovelock handed her. The baby, dumped hastily in her pram, stared at Laurie with solemn eyes.

'Your car's stuck in the ford?' Mrs Lovelock asked over her shoulder as she filled a kettle. 'You'll be the third this week, and my Ted not here to help you, he's out in the lower field ploughing. The phone's in the hall when you want it, I'll be making you a cup of tea.' She spoke in quick little jerks, the same way as she moved.

Laurie put up a secret prayer that Nick would be back from his calls and the one to take her message, but her luck was out; Julie fetched Dr Ross to the phone.

'What's all this?' His voice was clipped, impatient.

'I—I stalled the car in the middle of the ford. I'm at the farm now, but Mr Lovelock isn't here to help—he's out ploughing. I shall need a tow—' Laurie's voice trailed away, and she waited, her heart hammering painfully.

There was a pause, then he said in a completely expressionless voice, 'Is the car damaged?'

'No, it isn't,' she retorted, nervousness giving way to indignation, 'but I fell in the river!'

That didn't interest him; she heard the click

as he hung up. He wasn't going to waste any more time talking on the phone. In her mind she could see him stalking across to the stables, his face taut with anger. The prospect daunted her.

When she got back to the kitchen Mrs Lovelock had a chair drawn up to the Aga and a cup of tea ready for her. 'Is somebody coming to get you?'

'Yes—Dr Ross. Oh!' Laurie had remembered something.

'What's the matter?'

'I forgot to ask him to bring me a change of clothing. I'm still terribly wet.'

'Not to worry, Nurse, I can lend you something of mine. It'll hang on you like a sack, but it'll be dry. If you sit in those wet things much longer you'll catch a chill.'

This was sensible advice. Laurie had had a bit of a cold hanging about for days, but the recent sunny weather seemed to have cleared it up. She went upstairs with the farmer's wife and came down in a Crimplene skirt and a T-shirt which did rather resemble a potato sack upside down, but she was very grateful. Mrs Lovelock found her a plastic bag to put her wet things in.

She heard the sound of a car's engine and went to the door. Ross was approaching from the opposite direction so that he wouldn't have to tackle the ford, not that he could with any certainty, the Fiat being in the way.

With a deftness that she couldn't help but envy he backed his BMW up to the water's edge, then got out, went to the boot and lifted out a coil of rope. He had changed into breeches and boots and in no time had the Fiat roped to his own car—and he didn't even get wet. He could see Laurie standing on the step and she thought he would call her over to steer the smaller car, but he managed without her. He was back at his controls—the big car roared into life and began to edge forward and the Fiat followed. As soon as it was high and dry, he stopped, then got out of his own car and into the other. Laurie held her breath when he switched on the ignition; after two attempts the engine spluttered into life and she breathed again. Mrs Lovelock, who had been watching over her shoulder, discreetly disappeared when she saw Dr Ross striding up the path, and Laurie wished she could too.

'You blithering idiot!' he greeted her.

'I—I'm sorry,' Laurie faltered, too intimidated to stand up to such wrath.

'You'd be more sorry if you'd got water in the exhaust or into the engine—as it is you only stalled it; that's bad enough. Took the river at speed, I suppose?'

She nodded miserably.

'And you're the one who knows all about fords!' He glared at her, then seemed to relent a little. 'Did you hurt yourself when you fell?' And when she shook her head, 'I see Mrs

Lovelock has lent you something to wear.' She couldn't be sure but she thought she saw his lips twitch. 'I'd better go in and thank her.'

Laurie padded after him in her stockinged feet, finding both him and the farmer's wife bending over the pram looking at the sleeping baby. 'She's getting on fine,' Dr Ross said. 'I can see you don't need any further advice from me. How is little Emma settling down at school?'

'She loves it. She feels so important going off with her brother on the school bus every morning. Can I offer you a cup of tea, Doctor?'

'No, thank you, I must get along.' He turned to Laurie. 'You didn't lose the inhaler in the river, I hope?'

She pursed her lips, holding back words she would have uttered but for the presence of Mrs Lovelock. 'It's safe in the car—in my bag.'

'Good. Well, thank you again for taking such good care of my nurse, Mrs Lovelock.' He strode off and the two women followed him. At the door Mrs Lovelock said:

'I see you came the long way round to avoid the ford, Doctor.'

'Just as well. I wouldn't have been able to negotiate it with the other car in the way.'

Laurie's eyes flashed blue fire. 'Do you mean to say that there's actually another way to Lynch Green and you didn't tell me?'

He gave her a long hard look, then said contemptuously, 'You were so confident you knew how to cross a ford I didn't see the point. In any case, the other way is through a series of tortuous lanes—you would have only got lost.'

His assumption of her incompetence brought tears of rage to her eyes. 'You're an insufferable bully!' she burst out.

'I think I heard the baby,' said Mrs Lovelock, and vanished.

Dr Ross smiled grimly. 'I think we've embarrassed the good lady. I'll overlook it this time, Nurse, but don't call me names in front of my patients again; it's a sign of insecurity on your part, and I don't want their confidence in you undermined—'

'Stop it!' Laurie shouted at him. 'Stop belittling me—you do it all the time! Why can't you treat me with courtesy, like Nick—I mean Dr Lawrence—'

His eyes narrowed. 'I've seen the way Dr Lawrence treats you—that would be easy enough to copy, though I admit I haven't had the same practice he has. Where are you off to?' As she went to run from him he caught hold of her arm. 'Where are your shoes—did you lose them?'

'I-In the c-car—' Her tears had spilled over and were coursing down her cheeks. She sniffed and began hunting for her handkerchief, only to remember she had left it in the pocket of her dress. Dr Ross handed her his from his breast pocket.

'Here, mop yourself up—I should think

115

you're wet enough already without adding to it.' Suddenly, taking her completely unaware, he snatched her up into his arms, holding her like a child; holding her very close.

Now that she could look closely into his eyes she saw that the irises were rimmed with a darker band of grey, almost purple, and close to they didn't look so flinty as they did from a distance when he narrowed them. His eyebrows were well marked, very black, and his lips curved in a pleasing way. Not an ugly face at all, quite handsome in fact in a craggy way.

She pushed against his shoulders, trying to release herself, frightened that in some way he was going to show her he could outdo Nick Lawrence.

'Stop struggling, you little fool!' he snapped, tightening his hold. 'I'm only carrying you because you're not wearing shoes.' He dumped her into the driving seat of the Fiat. 'Now listen carefully. I'll give you instructions how to get home the long way round. For heaven's sake don't get lost—Dr Russett is waiting for you.'

'What about the inhaler for Mrs Lomax's father?'

'I'll deliver that.' Laurie handed it over to him in silence, then listened attentively as he gave her directions, memorising landmarks as he mentioned them. She could see Mrs Lovelock gaping at them from the farmhouse window and wondered whether she had seen the way she had been carried to her car. What a juicy bit of gossip that was for the village grapevine, but Laurie was too dispirited to get any amusement from the idea.

She followed the BMW through the hamlet until they came to a T-junction. Ross's arm shot out and he made signs that she was to take the left-hand lane, while he turned to the right towards Lynch Green.

She drove slowly, watching for a bank, a piece of broken walling, a dead elm tree, until she was finally on the road to Lower Wingfield and in familiar territory. Shirley was back from the dentist's by the time she got home, her cheeks crimson.

'Oh, poor you,' said Laurie when she saw her. 'Have you had fillings both sides?'

'I haven't had any fillings at all. Laurel Bush, what have you got on!'

Laurie plumped down in the nearest chair. Her head was aching and her throat was beginning to feel sore. 'Don't call me by that ridiculous name, you know how I hate it,' she said snappishly, then added quickly, 'Shirley, I'm sorry—but I've had the hell of an afternoon and I feel so groggy.'

As soon as Shirley was told the story she said, 'Bed for you. No way are you going to the surgery—I'll go and tell Dr Russett and offer to help out if necessary. You know you haven't fully recovered from a cold—you don't want to get a chill too.'

117

Dr Russett came over to see Laurie as soon as she heard about the ducking. Her quick eye noted the telltale signs of feverishness. 'Precaution is better than cure,' she said decisively. 'You should be in bed—see how you're shivering! Bed—an aspirin and a good night's sleep—could be an improvement in the morning. I can manage on my own this afternoon. Shirley, you stay here and see that she obeys orders.'

It was very pleasant being fussed over, Laurie reflected as Shirley tucked her up in bed. She hadn't had much of it in her life—it was she who had done the fussing, first for her grandfather and then the old ladies at the Beatrix Morse. In her darkened room the aspirins soon began to take effect and a delicious sense of drowsiness stole over her—it was a long time since she had slept during the day.

She awoke with a start, aware that someone was in the room with her. She tried to sit up, but a warm hand pressing gently against her shoulder pushed her back on her pillow. It was Nick.

'Just showing a professional interest,' he said soothingly. 'I've brought you something for a cough.'

'I haven't got a cough,' she protested.

'You will have if this chill settles on your chest.' He reached across the bed and opened the curtains. The sun had already set, leaving the sky a bowl of violet and gold, and by its light Laurie saw his eyes staring at her lips. Her heart started racing and she felt the colour seeping into her cheeks.

Nick smiled, easing himself into a comfortable position on the edge of her bed, then he took hold of her wrist and she could feel his thumb on her pulse.

'Galloping,' he said, his smile deepening. 'That could mean a fever, or—'

'Or what?'

His eyes held hers. 'Or a rapidly beating heart—I wonder why.' He leaned closer his eyes feasting on her. 'What enormous eyes you have, Laurie, great blue pools of light to trap any unwary male who looks into them. And such a tiny wrist—so fragile I feel I could snap it in two without any trouble.' His grip on her tightened. Behind him, through the partly-opened door, Laurie could hear Shirley in the kitchen. Up here they seemed in a private world of their own. She felt a delicious sense of awareness of Nick's nearness and her own precarious resistance. She knew he was going to take her into his arms and kiss her, that she was at present very vulnerable—but his nearness and her weakness made her reckless and she parted her lips on a tiny sigh.

Nick put one hand gently on her neck and bent his head to hers, then his lips began to seek her own. At first they were tender, warm, comforting, then they grew more demanding, becoming fiercely possessive. This way lay danger—she should make him stop—but she did not want him to.

'Oh, Nick, I love you—I love you,' she cried silently—though her silent cries sounded like screams in her throbbing head. She brought her hands up behind his neck and ran her fingers through his silky hair. She heard him groan and his hand moved from her neck to the opening of her nightgown. Now she pushed him away, but not before she saw the figure of a large man in the doorway. The last of the daylight illuminated him against the shadowy hallway, she saw the glint of his grey eyes, and the expression in them that sent a wave of blood all over her body. She gave a little gasp and stiffened, and Ross turned and went away as silently as he had come.

'What is it?' asked Nick, his voice low, urgent, his lips seeking hers again.

'Dr Ross—he saw us.'

'Damn!' Nick was immediately alert. He straightened up, looking over his shoulder. 'Are you sure?'

'Yes, he was in the doorway—he's gone now.' Laurie put out a hand in a gesture of submission, but he didn't see it. He got to his feet and went to the hall, staring down. He returned looking annoyed. 'Yes, I can hear him talking to Shirley. Damn! What's he doing here?'

'The same as you, perhaps—paying me a

professional visit.' She hadn't intended to sound so pert, but she was deeply hurt that Nick could change from lover to bystander with so little effort.

He frowned—then with a faint shrug of his shoulders he gave a rueful laugh. 'Yes, I deserved that—but Ross, with his nonconformist conscience, can be a pain in the neck over some things.' He came back to her bedside, lifted a hand to his lips and kissed it gently. 'You've had enough excitement for one day; what you need is sleep and lots of it. It's not private enough here to say all the things I'd like to say to you. Would you come out with me one evening, have dinner?'

He was the other Nick now, the caring doctor with the charming bedside manner—it was hard for her to gauge whether she loved both equally or one more than the other. 'I'd love that,' she said.

'That will be something to look forward to, then.' His eyes caressed her—a quick squeeze of her hand, and he was gone.

But paradoxically, when Laurie tried to compose herself for sleep once more it wasn't Nick's face that kept coming to mind but that of Ross Cramond. She couldn't forget the look in his eyes as he had stood in the doorway staring down at her. Accusing?—scornful?—contemplative? Yes, all that, but something else too—something akin to pity; and the idea of Ross pitying her filled her with unease.

CHAPTER SIX

In spite of every precaution the cold did settle on her chest, and Laurie was in a very low state of health for several days. At first lying in bed being waited upon, given soothing potions for her cough, was very comforting, but as soon as she began to feel better she also began to get bored. Dr Russett visited her every day, and once Laurie asked her when she could come back to work.

'Not until you've got rid of that cough—I don't want you spreading germs all over my patients. You just stay put until you're told you may get up.'

Laurie dreaded the days now—the long empty hours to do nothing but think of Nick and wonder why he hadn't been to see her again. Shirley let out the reason unwittingly when she was talking about a Dr Crowson who was now at the practice. 'Such a pet, one of the real old-fashioned family doctor types. He's locumed before when we've been shorthanded.'

Laurie stared, her eyes enormous in her pale face. 'Has Dr Ross gone away?' she asked hopefully.

'Not Dr Ross—didn't I tell you?' To cover her confusion Shirley made a great play of tidying the room which was already

122

scrupulously tidy, Mrs Crisp having been that morning. 'Dr Lawrence went away very suddenly. He took the rest of his annual leave—said he had business to attend to in London. Latest girl-friend, I shouldn't wonder,' she added under her breath, not meaning Laurie to hear, but she did. Laurie felt a coldness grip the base of her stomach.

Ever since Shirley had come to realise that Laurie's interest in Nick was becoming serious she had stopped referring to him in her half chaffing, half derogatory way. No more allusions to 'Golden Boy' or 'Heart-throb'. If she could possibly help it she didn't mention him at all except when she had to. She couldn't have made it more obvious that she didn't like him and didn't approve of Laurie liking him.

The silence went on. Laurie felt she had to break it or Shirley might hear the frightening thump of her heart.

'Perhaps he just felt like a holiday. He's been working very hard lately,' she said lamely.

'Well, I call it selfish, going off at twenty-four hours' notice—never mind who else is put out as long as he isn't!' Then Shirley saw Laurie's face and her scowl vanished. 'I'm sorry, Laurie, I'm just a bear with a sore head—and you not feeling well. What about a glass of hot milk with some nutmeg in it, that will help you sleep.'

But it didn't. Tormenting thoughts of Nick

kept Laurie tossing in her bed for hours. Why had he gone to London? Why hadn't he said anything to her about going? Every time she thought of the last occasion she had seen him she went hot with shame.

He had obviously been playing with her, and she had responded with such ardour that she must have seemed an easy conquest. No good telling herself that a combination of fever and drowsiness had blurred her judgment. She had wanted him to kiss her—perhaps if it hadn't been for Dr Ross's sudden appearance it might have gone further than kisses. What if it had— and he had walked out on her without another word? She buried her face in the pillow and gave way to bitter tears. So much for her grandfather's strict moral upbringing, how quickly she had lapsed when tempted; that was another thought to keep her awake—but the thought above all others that kept sleep at bay was the look of pity in Dr Ross's eyes. Just remembering it made her squirm. How he must be laughing at her, seeing her as another victim of Nick's charm! 'I won't think about it. I won't let it upset me,' she vowed, and cried harder than ever. She felt deflated, empty, drained of all emotion—and confused. She began to wonder what was upsetting her the most, Nick's offhandedness or Ross Cramond's pity.

The next day hunger got her out of bed. It was a good sign—she hadn't had a substantial meal for days. Shirley came tearing across the garden during her lunch break to see to Laurie's needs and stopped short at the kitchen door.

'My senses are not playing me false?' she queried hopefully. 'Do I smell lamb chops?'

'You do. I found them in the fridge, and I've made a Yorkshire pudding to go with them. Not usual, I know, but I'm hungry.'

'So am I,' said Shirley. 'I'm hungry for your Yorkshire pudding any time—and oh, what a change from eggs!' They had lived on eggs since Laurie's enforced rest.

Laurie was determined to get back into harness the next day, and she went across to see Dr Russett at Sinclair House before nine o'clock. The doctor was in her study with a breakfast tray on her desk and dealing with letters. She made Laurie sit down and have a cup of coffee with her.

'How's the cough?' she enquired.

'Much better. I want to start work again—' but even as she was speaking Laurie began to splutter into her handkerchief.

'It sounds it—but all right, I'll compromise with you. You can stay here and do some typing for me; I believe Ross wants some letters seen to too. I'll send Julie across with them. Will that keep you happy?'

Laurie had been hoping to get back to the surgery to get immersed in what she considered her real work—but Dr Russett's offer was better than nothing. Anything to take her mind off her inner pain. She didn't really want to be left alone, but alone with something to do was better than just being alone.

The morning went quickly—work had piled up while she was away and there was a backlog of correspondence and records to deal with. Every time Laurie looked up from her work she found herself staring at the photograph of a small boy that stood on the mantelpiece. He looked vaguely familiar, but she couldn't think of any small boys of her acquaintance that Dr Russett might also know. He was a serious little boy looking straight into the camera with large watchful eyes, a strand of very fair hair falling across his forehead. A handsome child.

Dr Russett came in soon after twelve o'clock to make herself some lunch, and Laurie took the opportunity to ask her about the photograph.

'Don't you recognise him? Take a closer look.'

Laurie went up to the mantelpiece—stared, then realised. It was the lock of hair that told her.

'Dr Ross—with fair hair!'

'Yes, when he was a child. That was taken on his fifth birthday, a few weeks before his mother bolted. I suppose she must still have had some feeling for him, because she took a copy of the photograph with her. Everything else she left—her clothes, her jewellery—just as if she didn't want to be beholden to her

126

husband any more. Well, I don't want to get back to that subject—I can think of better things to talk about than Linda Cramond. How about you, Laurie—you're looking much better, I must say. Perhaps work is a tonic for you. How would you like to run an errand to Lynch Green this afternoon? Yes, you've guessed it—Mrs Lomax's father again. Not another inhaler—he doesn't use them up that quickly—painkillers for his sciatica. Mrs Lomax says it's not vital, he can wait until we have the surgery there again, but I thought you might enjoy a run out.'

'Just as long as I go the long way round and avoid the ford,' said Laurie wryly.

'Yes, try to keep out of the river. We don't want you ill with double pneumonia next time!' Words that Laurie remembered with poignant misgiving later that afternoon.

She did not set off on her errand in the same lighthearted manner as she had a week ago. The shadow of Nick fell across her peace of mind. Even so, it was a treat to be out of doors again, and her coughing eased up in the open air.

As she drove past the market square she saw Mrs Coombe manoeuvring her car into the last free space outside the old Corn Hall, and waved. Mrs Coombe hadn't lost the four stone which Dr Ross had advised, but she was well on the way to it. In the past month her life had taken a surprising turn. Two days a week she

127

delivered meals on wheels, another day she helped at the Women's Guild stall in the market and the other two days she spent at a home for retarded girls giving them cookery lessons. Dr Russett had decided that voluntary work was the answer to Mrs Coombe's problem, and this was the outcome. She was doing a lot of cookery, which she loved—this time with her husband's approval—and she had stopped nibbling between meals, she was far too busy. Though everybody gave Dr Russett the credit for the change in Mrs Coombe Laurie had a smug feeling that it was she who had engineered it, though Dr Ross wouldn't admit, of course, that it was her outburst which had prompted it.

Now, thinking of Mrs Coombe, Laurie's mind went on automatically to Louise Fellowes, the only other private patient of Dr Ross she had met so far. Miss Fellowes still came regularly to the surgery, no better and no worse than the first time Laurie had seen her.

She often saw her about the town too—always in breeches or jeans, usually on her horse Cardinal. She seemed to care little about her appearance, yet she could look so attractive if she'd only take more trouble with herself, Laurie thought. She had learnt more about her background. Her father was a retired Colonel who managed the estate for the local squire. Not that the Honourable Robin Shipley was thought of as a squire in these days, but he was one of the largest landowners in the district, was much respected by his tenants, and had a beautiful wife who had been a former model.

'There's a traditional Christmas party at the Manor House every year; everyone from the practice is invited—we owe that bonus to Dr Ross; he was at school with the Hon. Robin,' Shirley had told her. She was the source of Laurie's information.

Just now Laurie couldn't get Louise Fellowes out of her mind. That tall, gangling girl who shambled along like an overgrown schoolboy, a look of utter desolation about her—was she an object lesson for unrequited love? Was that the snare waiting for her with her feelings for Nick Lawrence? Laurie shrugged off such a thought; no man was ever going to have that effect on her. What she found so incredible was that anyone could make themselves ill like that for love of Ross Cramond.

But once on the Lower Wingfield road, with the sky like a vast blue umbrella above and the honey-coloured stone walls racing alongside, her spirits began to rise. The inertia of the last few days fell away. Nick was due back on Monday—when they met again everything would be all right, she felt it in her bones.

Mrs Lomax tried to persuade Laurie to come in for a cup of tea. She was always glad to have someone to talk to—in fact her one failing was that she talked too much; her father, being deaf, wasn't much of a sounding-board. But Laurie saw danger in that; she'd never get away, and she had one other errand in mind. She wanted to call on Timmy Wilson. She knew his hand was better now, but she had missed the clinic that week and wanted to see him. She had some sweets for him in her pocket. She explained this to Mrs Lomax.

That good lady pursed her lips. 'I don't think you'll find anybody at home, Nurse. I saw Timmy going off with some bigger lads to collect conkers, then a bit later his mother went off to the shops.' There wasn't much that went on in Lynch Green that missed Mrs Lomax's keen eye.

Laurie thanked her and went on up the straggling High Road. The Wilson cottage stood gable end to the road. It belonged to a retired farmer who hadn't got the money or the inclination to put it in repair. From the outside it looked almost derelict, the one scar in the narrow street of neat stone cottages.

Laurie knocked several times, then gave up—there was nobody in. She stifled her disappointment. She'd grown fond of the impish Timmy and was going to miss his little red head bobbing round the door in the station waiting-room. She turned the car and drove down the hill again. Before she reached the road by the river she passed an embankment where two boys of ten or eleven were throwing pieces of stick at the branches of a horse-chestnut tree. She stopped the car and called over to them, asking if they'd seen Timmy Wilson.

'Aye, miss, he was with us, but he got kind of fed up an' went off on his own.'

'Back home, do you think?'

They shrugged, staring at her with blank faces. She realised then that she had interrupted a serious undertaking and they were waiting politely for her to go away.

Well, nothing for it then but to return to Merton, then she wondered if the mill was still open and serving teas—it was noted for its Banbury cakes. The afternoon was still young, the sun was warm, it could be very pleasant sitting by the river.

But she didn't reach the mill. She found Timmy, wedged amid some matted weeds and driftwood by the weir face downwards in the river.

She gave one wild look round—there was no one in sight—then was out of the car and struggling through the water towards the lifeless child. Her fingers were numb by the time she grasped hold of him and sobbing from exertion, half carrying him, half dragging, she got him to the river bank. His face was so white she thought he was already dead, his lips blue, his bright hair dark with water. She laid him face downwards on the grass, then turned his face to one side. She was relieved to see water trickling out of his mouth and nose, a sign that his air passages were clear—she felt in his mouth for any weeds that might choke him, but that was also clear; then she started artificial respiration. Kneeling by his side, she put her hands on the back of his ribs, pressing hard to expel air from his lungs, working in a slow steady rhythm to get him breathing again. After what seemed hours of hard work, but could only have been minutes, Timmy gave a tiny moan—then began to splutter feebly. Suddenly he brought up all the water he had swallowed, then crying, coughing, choking, he huddled against her, a frightened small boy minutes away from death.

Still nobody came along. Laurie couldn't wait any longer for help to materialise, so she picked Timmy up and carried him to her car. She had to get him to hospital immediately, he had been unconscious long enough to cause concern—but he was wet through, and so was she. The first priority was to get him dry. She thought of Mrs Lomax, and immediately made for her cottage.

It was Mrs Lomax's big day—she lived on the telling of its for weeks afterwards. Timmy was put into her own bed, a dressing-gown was found for Nurse, the son of her next-door neighbour was sent off to phone the surgery— and lastly, and very much as an afterthought because she had been forgotten in the heat of the moment, another neighbour sent to fetch Mrs Wilson.

Laurie was beginning to feel an overpowering sense of oppression by the time Dr Ross arrived. The heat in Mrs Lomax's small front room was fearsome. She constantly stoked the fire, piling on more coal, seeing Laurie's face getting redder and redder as a good sign—she didn't want any accusation of neglect put at *her* door. In any case, she wanted Nurse's clothes to dry, which they were doing very nicely, steaming away on the clothes-horse. She turned deaf ears to her father's complaints about the lateness of his tea coming from the back room. Little dramas like this were all too few in her life, and she was squeezing every ounce out of it.

Dr Ross went straight up to see Timmy and came down again carrying him wrapped in a blanket. He took him out to his car and placed him on the back seat, then came back to talk to Laurie—getting rid of Mrs Lomax by asking her to make Nurse a cup of tea.

Laurie looked up at him. She felt too tired even to straighten her shoulders. She crouched in the chair, shivering inwardly—not from cold or even nerves, but from the thought that a minute or two later and there would have been nothing she could have done for Timmy.

'I hope you're not going to make a habit of jumping in and out of rivers like this,' said Dr Ross with a bleak smile.

Laurie was in no mood to accept the challenge. She stared at him dully. 'How's

Timmy?' she asked.

'Sleeping. I can't examine him properly here, I'm taking him to the hospital. How do you feel?'

'I'm all right.'

He came over to her, felt her head, and then her pulse. 'You seem all right, but I advise you to go straight to bed when you get home. Will you be able to drive?'

'I said I'm all right,' Laurie answered impatiently. She turned her head away, she didn't want him to see her break down again.

He watched her keenly for a moment or two, then he said, 'Go on, have a good cry, it'll make you feel better. Even heroines can't keep a stiff upper lip indefinitely.'

She thought he was having a dig at her until she saw the expression in his eyes—was it compassion or that dreaded pity again? She turned her head quickly away, and he did a very unexpected thing as he passed, he squeezed her shoulder, very gently.

She heard Mrs Lomax see him to the door, heard him ask:

'What about the mother? Has she been told?'

'My neighbour's been looking all over for her, Doctor. She's not at home and she's not at the stores or the post office. If you ask me—'

'Well, when you see her tell her Timmy has been taken to Merton Cottage Hospital. Tell her gently, don't frighten her—it's going to be shock enough as it is,' and then Laurie heard Mrs Lomax give a very sceptical sniff which endorsed her own feelings exactly.

Laurie left about twenty minutes afterwards. Her clothes were almost dry, and she felt she couldn't stew in that overheated room for a minute longer; it was more likely to give her another chill than to prevent one. That there weren't any ill effects from her second ducking was mainly due to Shirley. She fell back on a remedy of her mother's—a hot mustard bath and then rum with hot milk, which she brought up to Laurie in bed.

'The phone's been busy this evening,' commented Laurie as she took the steaming mug.

'Reporters from the local papers; they want to come round and take photos of you.' Shirley grinned. 'What does it feel like to be a heroine?'

'Oh, don't! That's the second time I've been called that today—and it's so untrue. I only did what anyone else would have done. I knew I couldn't drown, the water isn't that deep. How is Timmy, have you heard?'

'He's being kept in the hospital for a few days. He's running a temperature, but I don't think it's causing too much concern.'

But the following morning brought sobering news. When Laurie reported at the surgery, and nothing would keep her away, Dr Russett told her that Timmy had developed bronchopneumonia and wasn't responding to antibiotics.

'We're keeping him at the Cottage Hospital for now,' Dr Russett went on, 'but if he gets any worse he'll have to be transferred to the District Hospital.'

It was a busy morning for Laurie. With the coming of autumn, colds and chests infections had proliferated; three expectant mothers came in for pregnancy tests and another was waiting for the result of hers. Laurie saw this last patient waiting at the dispensary—she turned and caught the eye of an older woman sitting in the waiting room. A look was exchanged between them—a look of such rapture on the younger woman's face as she did the thumbs-up sign that Laurie felt tears prick her eyes. There was one satisfied patient in the Merton surgery that morning at least!

She had already made up her mind to go and see Timmy during her lunch-break. She wanted to take him something, but sweets were now out of the question; a colourful picture-book seemed the best present for a small boy confined to bed.

There was a bookshop in Merton High Street, and she didn't take long choosing—a book caught her eye in the shop window. 'The latest Timmy book by well-known children's author,' said the promotion display above the book—'*Timmy and the Wooden Horse*', another favourite to add to the list of Timmy books.'

Well, there it was—what child could resist seeing his own name in print, and there were other books in the series she could add as presents later. Laurie went into the shop, made her purchase and had it wrapped.

Less than ten minutes later she was parking the Fiat in the hospital forecourt. She saw Ross's BMW already there and hoped she wouldn't run into him, or Matron either. Her dealings with Matron hadn't always been of a friendly nature—not on the older woman's part. Laurie had to admit she was an efficient nurse, but she wasn't a very nice human being. She sucked up to her superiors and bullied those under her, not admirable qualities in one in a position of responsibility.

The hospital had that quiet brooding air that sometimes took over during the interval between the serving of lunches and visiting time. Laurie met nobody as she crossed the hall and mounted the stairs to the children's ward. Even that was quiet, which was unusual. But only three cots were occupied and the occupants of two of those were asleep.

Timmy wasn't in that ward—he had been put in a small room reserved for infectious cases or patients needing special attention. The door to that stood partly open, and as Laurie approached she heard someone talking. Thinking it was one of the nurses, she pushed the door open further—then paused. It wasn't a nurse in there. It was Lucy Wilson, on her knees beside the bed, staring with naked anguish at the unresponsive figure of her small son.

She was speaking aloud, not praying as much as pleading. 'Don't let him die, please, Lord—please spare him. I love him so much—give me another chance. I'll be a better mother to him in future, I promise I will. Oh, God, please let him live—he's such a little boy—he's too young to die!'

She didn't see Laurie or even hear her as with a choking cry she backed out of the room. Laurie turned, blinded by tears, and stumbled out of the ward, down the staircase and through the downstairs hall. She was dimly aware that she passed Dr Ross with Matron and that they both stared after her with startled faces, but she went blindly on until at last she was in her car with her head bowed on the steering wheel, letting her tears flow unchecked.

Poor, poor Lucy Wilson—how she had wronged her! Sluttish, indolent, careless—yes, she was all that, but she was also caring and she did love Timmy—only a mother with a caring heart could suffer such an extremity of grief.

Laurie raised her head wearily and wiped the tears from her cheeks with her open hand. She looked unseeing at the package in her other hand and dropped it on the seat beside her. As she turned the key in the ignition she paused, struck by another thought.

If she had been so wrong about Lucy Wilson couldn't she have been just as wrong about Ross Cramond?

CHAPTER SEVEN

That afternoon, before going across to Sinclair House for a session with Dr Ross, Laurie put through a call to the Cottage Hospital to enquire after Timmy. The news was good and she decided to visit him again at the first opportunity. She was also told his mother was still with him.

It was a long afternoon and a busy one; there were two new patients to be registered. Both had lengthy histories of past illnesses, and by the time Laurie had entered all their particulars in the record book Louise Fellowes had arrived for her regular check-up.

As usual she was the last patient to be seen, an arrangement Laurie thought more contrived than accidental. She looked different this afternoon; for one thing she was in a skirt and a very expensive-looking pale blue sweater. The pencil-line skirt accentuated her thinness, the blue sweater made her skin look even more sallow, yet there was a winsomeness about her frailty. Laurie could see why Ross was attracted to her.

As soon as she had put Louise's file on the

desk Laurie returned to her own room, waiting to be summoned if needed. There was always some bookwork to get on with. Presently she heard the sound of a car driving off—Louise had borrowed her father's Land Rover—then Ross buzzed for her.

He was reclining on the windowsill, hands deep in his trouser pockets, staring abstractedly at the toes of his shoes. He looked up as Laurie entered and she thought there was a tiredness about him, particularly in his eyes. But then he never spared himself where his patients were concerned.

'What do you make of Miss Fellowes?' he asked unexpectedly.

'She doesn't eat enough,' she answered without thinking.

He grunted and shifted his positon. 'That's obvious—but why? Come along, let me hear why you think she isn't eating.'

Laurie was flattered but at the same time flustered by his command. 'I thought it was a straightforward case of anorexia nervosa.'

He began to stalk about the room, jingling the loose change in his pockets. 'Yes, yes, the easy answer—we all think that. But what brought the condition on in the first place? That's what I've got to find out.'

'I know what I think, but you might not like the answer,' she said, greatly daring.

'Try me.'

'She may be suffering from unrequited love.'

He gave a grim laugh. 'You think that too, eh?' He didn't enlarge on that, and she noticed that he didn't ask who she thought Louise was in love with either. Perhaps he knew. She felt uncomfortable beneath his gaze; he was staring at her in a very fixed way.

'Have you any personal experience of unrequited love?' he asked lightly enough, but there was a steel-like intensity about his words that brought the colour to her cheeks.

Laurie didn't answer him. She picked up the files that were lying on his desk, sorting them out in alphabetical order ready to take back to her own room, but he barred the way.

'I said, have you ever had any personal experience of unrequited love?'

She forced herself to meet his gaze, giving him look for look. 'I don't think you have any right to ask me that,' she said quietly.

A shadow of a smile played about his lips. 'It's in the interests of medicine only, my dear Nurse,' he said. 'I was thinking entirely of Louise Fellowes and how we could help her. *You* brought up the subject of unrequited love, so I thought you might know something about it.'

Her discomfiture grew. His teasing words were too near the bone, but he couldn't know that. Or did he—did he suspect what she felt for Nick and was this his way of confirming it? Did he really believe she would confide in him, considering the coldness that existed between

141

them?

She had finished tidying her own room and was about to leave when he came in to her. 'Look, we've both had a heck of an afternoon; I'm dog-tired and I know you must be. What about joining me upstairs for a cup of tea?'

Laurie was so surprised she practically gaped at him. The great Dr Ross inviting her to his flat for a cup of tea—she couldn't believe it! Her instinct told her to refuse, but there was a look in his eyes that made her heart flutter in an annoying way, and in an effort to cover up her confusion she found herself accepting.

He led the way up the wide sweep of the staircase and ushered her into a room immediately above the room that had once been his mother's—but the size and shape were the only similarities. There was no silk or damask or fine antiques in this room, and there was no mistaking it was a man's room either. There were deep armchairs and wide bookcases, a music centre, and a rolltop desk. There was not a sign of chinz or of any flowers. There was, however, a trolley laid ready for tea with an electric kettle nearby, and it didn't escape Laurie's notice that it was set with two of everything. So Ross's sudden invitation had not been on the spur of the moment—this had been planned. She found it hard to believe that he could intrigue her in this way, but now she found herself looking at him with renewed interest. He *was* handsome in a rugged out-of-doors sort of way, and the eyes that she always thought of as cold as slate were really a remarkable colour. They changed with his moods; in his mellow moments such as now they were nearly blue.

She had refused his offer of one of the deep chairs, knowing it would swallow her up, and had perched instead on an upright one by the window. From there she could look over the wide vista of the Cotswold hills. Autumn was beginning to take over, subtly changing the colours of the landscape, bringing the riper hues of gold and orange and russet to the uplands, and in the distance the sky was lavender-coloured.

'Admiring the view?' Dr Ross stood beside her, a cup of tea in one hand and a plate of cakes in the other. 'Well, feast your eyes on this plate of Mrs Crisp's goodies instead. I can guarantee every one of them.'

'Oh no, I don't want anything to eat, thank you.' She took the cup from him. 'I promised Shirley I'd make a spaghetti bolognaise for supper, so I must leave room for it.'

'I've been told about your cooking. Perhaps you'd invite *me* to supper one evening and let me judge for myself.'

Such a suggestion filled her with alarm. She didn't see it as a compliment. Entertain Ross Cramond? She knew she would drop every dish as she took it from the oven—the sauce would curdle, the pastry, if any, would turn out like leather. In short she'd make the same hash of it as she had of her practical—just because he would be looking on. She didn't have to say no, her face said it for her, and abruptly Ross turned away, replacing the cakes on the trolley in an impatient manner.

'I can see the idea doesn't appeal to you,' he said coldly. 'I didn't realise I would make such an unwanted guest.'

Laurie felt wretched. Inhospitality wasn't one of her failings, but she didn't feel sure enough of herself or Ross to meet him yet on a social basis. She tried to explain, blurting out, 'Oh no, it isn't that. You don't understand—' when the phone cut her short. Ross picked up the receiver.

He listened without commenting, said, 'Thank you, Julie,' and replaced the instrument. He looked across at her, grim-faced, his eyes grey once more.

'That was a message from your friend Nick,' he said sarcastically. 'He's catching the eight o'clock train this evening.'

Laurie, caught off her guard, half rose from her chair, and the cup she was holding tipped into the saucer, shooting the tea all over the carpet. She stared in horror, wondering how such a small cup could hold so much liquid as the stain spread, then she was down on her knees mopping it up with her handkerchief.

Ross immediately pulled her to her feet again. 'Leave that,' he ordered. 'Mrs Crisp will see to it.' He was angry, not because of the accident, she realised, but because of the way she had reacted. She must have looked stupid grovelling at his feet using an inadequate square of cotton on a sizeable pool of hot tea. Tears of frustration and self-rage pricked at her eyes, but she blinked them back, determined not to cry in front of him. She felt humiliated enough as it was—something even the joyful news of Nick's homecoming could not lessen.

'Let me replenish your cup,' Ross said more kindly. 'I don't think you got any tea from that one.'

'No, I must get back—I must go—there's chores to do.' She walked blindly to the door and hearing him following said quickly, 'I can see myself out, don't bother.'

She didn't feel safe until the door was closed behind her and she was hurrying down the stairs. The tears came then. She felt such an utter incompetent fool. What a way to behave! First spilling her tea, then trying to mop it up— just like a selfconscious schoolgirl invited out to tea for the first time. But this was the effect Ross had on her—making her feel inadequate, and to use one of her grandfather's words, gauche.

There was a letter on the mat at the cottage which had been delivered by hand, as it had no stamp. It was addressed to her in an unknown writing, so when she had opened it she turned to the signature first. It was from Lucy Wilson.

Dear Nurse,

I want to thank you for saving Timmy's life. Dr Ross told me all about it, and so did Mrs Lomax. I can't bear to think what might have happened to him if you hadn't driven past when you did. I know you don't think much of me as a mother, but believe me, Timmy means everything to me. If anything happened to him I think I'd kill myself. I know I've got a rotten temper and I get impatient, especially with kids, but that doesn't mean I don't love him. I was out looking for him in the woods that day he fell in the weir. I haven't any family of my own. I was brought up in a Home, and I didn't know my husband very long before we got married. He died soon afterwards, so I didn't get to know any of his folks, if he had any—he never said. I'm not much of a letter writer, I don't get much practice, but I hope you'll call in to see us the next time you're in Lynch Green.

Yours truly, Lucy Wilson.

Laurie's eyes were wet again as she folded the letter; it made her feel very humble. Those few grateful words had touched the depths of her being and in some subtle way helped to

146

alleviate the humiliation she had inflicted upon herself at Sinclair House. It's strange the way we misjudge people, she told herself, thinking of Lucy Wilson. How was it then that once again an image of Ross Cramond came to her mind just then?

Shirley decided to have an early night that night, but Laurie felt restless and sat up to write letters. She owed one to Sadie, but her heart wasn't in it and she pushed it away unfinished. Her mind was on the telephone all the time, willing it to ring. Surely Nick had arrived back by now? Wouldn't he call her to tell her he was home, to enquire after her? At half-past twelve she gave up hope and started for bed—and then came the awaited *burr-burr, burr-burr*. She rushed to the phone and picked it up.

'Hallo—hallo!' she cried eagerly.

But it was Ross who answered.

'I saw your light was still on, otherwise I wouldn't be calling at this hour. I forgot to give you a message. There'll be a patient calling in tomorrow morning at eight-thirty for a blood-test. He can't manage any other time.'

Her disappointment that the call wasn't from Nick came through in her voice no matter how she tried to disguise it. She said dully, 'I'll be there in time.'

'Thank you.' Then, brusquely, 'Good night.' Ross hung up. This time Laurie didn't loiter, she was anxious to get to bed, to get this day over—it hadn't been an auspicious one.

* * *

Promptly at eight-thirty the following morning Laurie walked across to the surgery to keep the appointment with Mr Burge. He was one of the local greengrocers and she knew him by sight— a large red-faced man who spent his leisure moments, and there weren't many of those, on the bowling green. Lately he had been suffering from cramp, especially at night, and Dr Ross had suggested a blood test to discover if his body was lacking in potassium.

Early as Laurie was, Mr Burge was before her. She unlocked the door and let him in. 'Sorry to get you up so early, Nurse,' he said in his jokey, goodhumoured way, 'but I'm catching the nine-thirty train up to Town. Will you be finished with me by then?'

'Oh yes, this won't take long.' Laurie led the way into the treatment room. Sometimes big men were the worst patients as far as having injections were concerned, but Mr Burge didn't come into that category. He watched Laurie's proceedings with interest, and made the usual quip when she siphoned his blood into a small bottle, 'Well, I haven't got any blue blood in my veins, that's a fact. What happens now?'

'Your blood will be sent to the District Hospital for analysis and we'll notify you of the results.'

Mr Burge rolled down his shirt-sleeve. 'Well, thank you, Nurse, you've been very gentle with me. There's a consignment of fresh peaches coming in this morning, I'll ask the missus to pick some out for you. Just come along and collect them any time.'

Laurie was always touched by the generosity of the patients. They would love to give gifts, even if it were just flowers or produce from their gardens. She saw Mr Burge off the premises, watching him as he walked away with the limp, a legacy from the Burma campaign. Then, as she had missed breakfast, she went to the kitchen to make some coffee. She heard someone behind her and thinking it was Shirley, said, 'Care for a cup of coffee?'

'There's something I'd like much better,' said a voice she knew so well.

Laurie spun round, her face lighting up with joy. Nick home again, and looking handsomer than ever! The week's absence had imbued him with a kind of radiance, intensifying the look in his eyes. She had meant to meet him with coolness; she reminded herself that he had gone away without a word of goodbye—that she couldn't allow him to think it was just a question of 'whistle and I'll come to you'—but all her good intentions went by the board at the sight of him. She was no good at pretence, and it *was* good to see him again.

She smiled, her dimples flashing. 'Had a good holiday?'

'I haven't been on holiday.' He took the coffee mug away from her and twisted her round so that he had only to lower his head for his lips to reach hers and to kiss her in a way that both possessed her and reassured her at the same time.

He did love her! Of course he loved her!

'What are you doing tonight?' he whispered, his cheek pressed against hers.

'I promised to go to the cinema with Shirley.'

'Put her off—you can go to the flicks any old time. Tonight is special. I've got something very important booked for tonight. That dinner date you promised me—say yes, and I'll take you to the Blue Cedar.'

The Blue Cedar, once The Cedars and a private residence, was now an exclusive country club. It was very expensive, and Laurie was aware that this outing was not just an ordinary date—Nick had something more important in mind. A celebration, perhaps? Her heart bounded, and Nick kissed her again. 'I can see it's a "yes,"' he said. 'See you at seven-thirty, then.'

Only when he had gone did she realise that Shirley was on the hall side of the kitchen door and must have heard every word. And she didn't look too pleased.

'Don't mind me,' she said tartly. 'I can go to the films on my own!'

'Please don't take it like that. How could I refuse him?' Laurie was contrite.

'I didn't expect you to refuse. After all, how often do you get the chance to eat at the Blue Cedar?'

Laurie was baffled. It was not like Shirley to be sarcastic. 'I'm not going for the sake of a good meal!' she protested

'The more's the pity—I wish you were. The worst you could get from that is indigestion. Goodness knows what to expect from Nick—'

'You've never liked him,' interrupted Laurie heatedly. 'Right from the beginning you've tried to put me off him. You're like a dog in a manger!'

Shirley went white. 'Think that if you want to,' she snapped, and stalked away. Laurie ran after her, pulled her round and hugged her.

'Please, Shirley, don't be angry with me—I didn't mean to say that. I'm so excited and so happy and so mixed up. I'd be happier still if you could only like Nick. I more than like him, Shirley—I love him, and I believe he loves me. I think he intends to ask me to marry him when he takes me to the Blue Cedar tonight.'

Laurie's blue eyes were so eager-looking, so beseeching that Shirley's heart melted. 'And you *will* marry him, of course?'

'Just give me half a chance!'

They heard a footstep behind and both turned to see who it was. Dr Ross was on his way to his room. Laurie dragged Shirley into Reception. 'Do you think he heard?' she whispered.

'Does it matter? He must know about you and Nick, anyway—he'd have to be blind and deaf not to.' Shirley's sudden warm smile broke out. 'I'm sorry for the way I snapped at you, Laurie. I was looking for you to give you this letter. It came after you left.'

Laurie took the letter, recognising the writing immediately.

'Would you believe it, it's from Sadie, and I was only writing to her last night. Perhaps it's as well I didn't finish.' She scanned the closely-written pages. 'Goodness, she's excited—she's pregnant—how lovely for her! She wants me to go and visit before, she says, she gets as big as a house.'

'Then I would if I were you. By the way, when are you taking your re-sit?' asked Shirley.

'Some time in November, but don't talk about it. The very thought sends shivers down my back.' The weeks were slipping by and Laurie thought of all the revision yet to do. She had already filled in the application form and sent it off, but had told nobody—not even Dr Russett. She was superstitious about discussing the exam, as if it were tempting fate.

'It occurred to me,' Shirley was saying, 'that you would need somewhere to stay in London then, so why not with Sadie and John?'

Laurie laughed. 'I'd already got that little scheme worked out, and was trying to get around to it in my letter last night.' She gave a happy sigh. 'This has been a lovely day so far—

nothing but good news—makes up for yesterday, which was a disaster. I must dash, Dr Russett will be waiting—'

Shirley watched Laurie hurrying away to the doctor's room and sighed also, but not happily. I hope it does remain good for you, pet, she thought. But I've got my doubts.

It had started to drizzle by lunchtime. Laurie looked up at the sky as she backed the Fiat along the drive of Sinclair House. She was going over to the Cottage Hospital to see Timmy; she knew she wouldn't be able to go out and enjoy herself that evening without satisfying herself how he was progressing.

He was being tucked down for his afternoon nap when she arrived. The nurse in charge recognised her and nodded. 'You've come to see this young man? We're very pleased with him. He's a good boy—he's eaten most of his dinner and now he's going to sleep.'

'I promise I won't stay long,' Laurie answered. Even twenty-four hours had made a difference to Timmy. There was colour in his cheeks again and his eyes, through heavy with sleep, had a brightness about them. He grinned at her.

'Have you brought me a present?' he croaked in a husky voice. He had been quick to notice the package in her hand. 'Can I open it?' He looked at the older nurse.

She shook her head. 'Not now—when you wake up. I think you've had quite enough

153

presents for one day already.' She bent over the bed, then looked up at Laurie. 'He's off. He nearly fell asleep over his pudding. He's made a remarkable recovery. I hope he'll never forget that he owes his life to you.'

Laurie felt embarrassed—she had had to face a volley of similar remarks since the story had been made public. She gave a selfconscious smile. 'Oh, it was nothing, anyone would have reacted the same way. Isn't Timmy's mother here any longer?'

They walked out of the side ward together. 'She's still with us,' said the nurse. 'Having some lunch herself, I hope. I told her that if she didn't let up for a minute or two we'd have another patient on our hands, and we're short-staffed enough as it is. That was the only way I could prise her away from the bedside. Why? Did you want to see her?'

Laurie thought of the letter in a drawer at the cottage. 'I was hoping to see her, but I won't intrude on her now. Tell her I called, will you?'

She tripped down the stairs and out of the main door. It was raining heavily now, but she didn't notice—she was too happy to let a little thing like rain dampen her spirits.

She was in the shower that evening when she heard the doorbell, and when she came out of the bathroom Shirley handed her a cellophane gift box marked with the name of a local florist.

'I'll say this much for Nick Lawrence, he

154

knows how to do things in style,' she commented drily.

In the box was a single pink rose. Laurie smiled.

'Well, this has solved one problem for me. I didn't know whether to wear my white blouse or my pink with the black velvet skirt. It will have to be the pink, it's almost the same colour.'

Nick called at seven-thirty, hooting for Laurie from the roadway. The rain had eased up a little, but Shirley still insisted on escorting her out to the car under an umbrella. She thought Laurie mad for not wearing a coat.

As they drove off Dr Ross appeared from the house opposite, the faithful Fergus at heel. He didn't notice Shirley, he was too intent on watching the disappearing car. It wasn't light enough to see by his expression the thoughts passing through his mind at that moment, but he squared his shoulders and strode off into the rain like a man who had come to a decision.

CHAPTER EIGHT

For some time afterwards Laurie couldn't remember what she ate that night; at the time it tasted like ambrosia. At first she was overawed by the gilt and white dining-room, but the waiters were so helpful that she soon felt at ease. On a dais in the corner a string quartet played romantic music from another era. Nobody was dancing, most diners seemed contented enough just to dine and listen. Nick suggested they had their coffee and liqueurs in the lounge, and she followed him there to a table screened by a stone pillar. A huge log fire burned in the original hearth, filling the room with a pungent smell of autumn. It had started to rain heavily again, Laurie could hear it drumming on the windowpanes.

Nick looked flushed—the fire or too much to drink? Laurie had restricted herself to one glass and had refused the port. It wasn't that she didn't like drink, but it quickly went to her head. She noticed that other diners had been equally abstemious, perhaps thinking of the drink-and-drive laws. She wondered at Nick as he downed his second brandy.

'Aren't you worried about the breathalyser test?' she asked with some concern.

He grinned at her. 'I'm not troubled about that. By the time I leave here I shall be quite sober.'

Laurie was disturbed by that remark, hoping he wasn't intending to stay too late, because they both had full sessions the following day. They were sharing an upholstered window seat, and now he moved closer, slipping an arm round her. She could smell the brandy on his breath.

'Don't draw away from me,' he said. 'If you

only knew how I've missed you—how I've longed to get back to you. You're like fire in my blood. No, more than fire—an infection.' He started to muzzle her ear in a maudlin way, making her feel embarrassed. An elderly couple at a nearby table were staring disdainfully.

'Nick, don't do that—not here,' she pleaded.

'Of course not here, it's far too public,' he laughed. 'But there is another room booked for us—upstairs.'

Laurie stared at him, her mind racing. 'You mean a private sitting-room?'

'Nothing less than a suite, Little Tree. Tonight we're celebrating.'

She had guessed aright, then. Her heart began to pound. 'Celebrating, Nick?'

'Of course. Why do you think I booked a table for two and a suite for the night?'

Laurie gave a little gasp and put her hand on her throat. She could feel a pulse beating. This was what she had been hoping and praying for—Nick to ask her to marry him. But not like this; not with his face flushed and his speech slurred. It was taking the pleasure out of a moment that should have been very beautiful.

He was so close to her she could see miniature portraits of herself reflected in each pupil. She had dressed her hair in a new style for the occasion, piled it on top and encircled the thick black knob with a slender gold chain. All this she could see clearly, and overlaying it a look in Nick's eyes that intimidated her.

'Come upstairs—now,' he said urgently.

Would it be wrong to anticipate marriage? It went against all the tenets of her grandfather's teaching, but *he* had belonged to another time, another world. She loved Nick and he loved her. He wanted to marry her—where was the wrong?

He clung to her as they climbed the stairs, unsteady on his feet. They passed a young chambermaid who quickly turned her head, but not quickly enough. Laurie saw the smile and felt cheapened by it. The suite was on the first floor. As Nick fumbled with the key, Laurie took it from him, fitted it into the lock and pushed open the door.

It was a beautiful room; there were so many flowers in it it looked like the bridal suite. Nick must have spent a fortune. A bottle of champagne ready in a bucket of ice carried on with the bridal theme. No doubt in the bedroom beyond there would be more flowers—perhaps even more champagne. No expense had been spared, Nick had taken it for granted that this was to be their honeymoon. Was it because he had taken it for granted that she felt neither flattered or thrilled?

He came behind her, put his arms round her and drew her near, but impatiently she broke away. He wasn't annoyed—just amused.

'What's the matter?' he demanded.

'I—I don't like being taken unawares. I

didn't expect this—' she indicated the room. 'You only mentioned dinner. I didn't come prepared to stay the night. I haven't even got a toothbrush.'

He roared with laughter. 'A toothbrush? You care about a toothbrush at a time like this? Don't worry, you'll find everything necessary in there,' he nodded towards the bathroom. 'Have some champagne. Two glasses of this, my love, and you won't care a damn.'

'But I want to care. To all intents and purposes this is my wedding night. It's important to me.'

Nick blinked at her, still rocking slightly, the bottle clasped in both hands. 'Wedding night?' he repeated.

'I know we're not actually married, but that will come later, you said so. It's quite the thing now to do—this, I accept that, but I do wish— Oh, Nick, if only you could have been a little more patient!'

He carefully replaced the champagne, then flopped into a chair as if rid of some burden. He stared at her in a stupid kind of way. 'Look, I don't actually remember what I said, but I'm pretty damn sure I didn't mention marriage. Marriage isn't in my plans—not for years.'

Laurie felt the blood drain from her face. The chilling sensation went on and on as if her blood was flowing out of her body altogether, leaving her empty of all feeling. She returned Nick's look, appalled at his indifference. 'You said this was a celebration. I thought you meant us becoming engaged.'

'Oh dear, we *have* got our wires crossed!' He blinked again, then smiled, patting the seat beside him. 'Come and sit here and let's talk things over. Come and have a drink.' It was his panacea for all ills.

She could see it didn't affect him in the slightest her being so upset. Had she been wrong about him being in love with her? What she had mistaken for love went by another word. She felt bitterly betrayed.

'You got me here under false pretences,' she said accusingly.

'Oh, for goodness' sake! Not the tragedy queen act.' Nick struggled to his feet. 'Little Tree, this is the nineteen-eighties, not the eighteen-eighties, though they had their fun on the side too, but not as openly as we do. Step into the twentieth century with me, Laurie, you'll find it fun.' And he held out his hand beguilingly.

'I don't care for that kind of fun.' Her voice broke. It wasn't easy to keep up such anger when she was feeling so hurt. 'I thought you loved me—'

He stumbled towards her. 'But I do love you. I adore you. Every time you flash your dimples at me, my pulse begins to race. Dear Little Tree—'

'And stop calling me by that ridiculous name! You don't know how—*infantile* it sounds!'

Nick widened his eyes. 'Wow, you are prickly all of a sudden! I'm only suggesting having this one lovely night together because I won't be in this country for much longer.'

Laurie was too stupefied to answer, but he didn't appear to notice that. He went on exultantly, 'I've been offered a job in a fashionable New York clinic. It's no secret in Merton that I've been looking around to better myself for some time now, but I didn't dream I'd pull off anything like this. I was summoned for an interview in London at very short notice, and then was kept waiting some days for the result. I scooted back here as soon as I got the good news—and now you've spoilt it all!' He pouted, perhaps deliberately, but all the same Laurie found it jarred.

So that air of suppressed excitement which she had mistaken for radiance was on account of the successful outcome of his visit to London—not the fact of seeing her again. With a will-power she didn't realise she possessed she braced herself to ask him how long he had before taking up his new appointment.

'A month. I should have given Ross three months' notice, but he waived that. He knows chances like this don't grow on trees.'

So Ross knew—and possibly Dr Russett and Dr Crowson too—but not Shirley. She knew more than the others what Nick meant to her. Shirley would have warned her.

Suddenly Nick took a step nearer and caught her roughly in his arms. 'Don't play hard to get, my pet. Let's enjoy our time together. You won't regret it I promise you.'

He was so sure of himself—so sure of her. Laurie struggled and broke free.

'It's just a game to you, isn't it?' she stormed at him. 'I'm just your latest plaything. Shirley tried to warn me, but I wouldn't listen. Well, Dr Lawrence, you'll have to get yourself another playmate to fill in your time until you leave for America. This one doesn't play those kinds of games!'

She made a dash for the door, but he was there before her. There was an ugly look on his face. 'You don't know the rules. Marriage—is that all you think of? Marriage and babies and the kitchen sink—is that what you want?'

She was shaking but resolute as she faced him. 'No, I want a man who will love me and be loyal to me, who will stand before the altar and make marriage vows with me—and if that includes babies and the kitchen sink, then I'll rejoice!'

He couldn't hold her gaze, his eyes dropped and he stood back to let her go, not quite drunk enough to keep her against her will. In the fleeting glance she gave him before she ran she looked for some sign of remorse, but saw only a cynicism that bewildered her.

She dashed down the stairs and through the foyer, only stopped in her mad flight by the commissionaire. 'It's raining hard, madam. Shall I call a taxi?'

Too late she remembered she had left her handbag in the suite—but nothing would induce her to return for it. She wasn't thinking coherently, she could have taken a taxi and paid the other end, but she ran out into the rain not caring.

It was a five-mile walk back to Merton. She had gone less than a mile before she was drenched to the skin and regretting her mad impulse, regretting not bringing a coat, regretting meeting Nick—even regretting ever coming to Merton.

She was at her lowest ebb when she heard a car overtaking her—the first she had seen since leaving the Blue Cedar. She immediately thought it was Nick coming after her and drew back under the trees. But even in the dusk she could make out the outline of the BMW. The passenger door was flung open and Ross said, 'You'd better come in out of the rain.'

Laurie was never more pleased to see him, and she didn't stop to wonder what he was doing at this time of night in a lonely lane. She climbed into the car and he reached across for the car-rug in the back. 'Here, drape this round you,' he said, and after a pause added, 'I've given up expecting to rescue you in a dry condition.'

As warmth slowly surged through her, the numbness, both physical and mental, that had gripped her began to thaw, bringing in its wake a sense of complete exhaustion. She was grateful to Ross for his silence. He hadn't spoken since that first quiet command. He looked grimly ahead, concentrating on his driving as he steered the big car through the rain-washed lanes. Presently the lights of Merton appeared like smudged images in the rain. The car purred along the High Street, then turned into the Green and came to a stop outside the cottages.

Ross seemed reluctant to let her go. Looking straight ahead, his hands idle on the wheel, he said, 'I gather Nick must have told you about his New York job?' What he didn't say and she was sure he was thinking, was—'Did you quarrel? Was that why you were running away?'

He must have heard her telling Shirley about her date with Nick and her conviction of a proposal of marriage—otherwise why mention Nick? There was no point in hiding anything now. With some bitterness, she said, 'Yes, and we quarrelled, and I ran away. Not because he's going to America, but because he *presumed* I would stay the night with him.'

'And of course you wouldn't.' There was a suppressed anger about him that was not directed at her.

Laurie was very tired and near to tears, but she was able to control her voice. 'No. I'm not that kind of girl, I'm afraid.'

Ross gave a short laugh. 'There's no need to

be afraid about it!'

'What I meant was—Nick thinks I'm old-fashioned. He asked me to step into the twentieth century with him, whatever he means by that. But he didn't ask me to marry him, and as you must know, I was expecting him to. That was why I ran away—and now you can laugh at me!'

'My dear child, I have no wish to laugh at you,' he said gravely, and Laurie found it comforting to be called a child at that moment.

'Well, thank you for the lift,' she said awkwardly, not quite knowing how to take her leave of him. 'It was a lucky chance for me you came along when you did. I'd left my handbag in the hotel and I didn't want to go back for it.'

Ross gave another grim laugh. 'So you were prepared to walk home in flimsy clothes in pouring rain! Look, I don't want you off sick again. Take tomorrow off and stay in bed.'

She was nearly tempted—not for the chance of having a day in bed, but to put off the awful moment of having to face Nick again. But it was the easy way out and she'd have to face him eventually. 'No, thanks, I'll be all right.' Ross opened the door for her and she stepped out. 'I'll dry this rug off for you and give it back. And your handkerchief—I haven't returned that yet.'

'I lent it to you on another occasion when you were rather damp, I believe.' In the dark his eyes glittered and she felt he was smiling.

There was amusement in his voice. 'Oh, Laurie, you and your duckings!—what a girl! Go on off with you and get out of those wet things.'

Laurie didn't hesitate. She ran round the back of the cottage and went in by the kitchen door. An astonished Shirley, wearing her plastic apron saying—'Don't shoot the cook—she was doing her best', and with two large rollers in her hair, stared at her dumbfounded.

'Laurel Bush! Have you fallen in the river again?'

'Shirley, if you have any thought for me at all, don't ask me any questions, don't ask me to explain—just give me until tomorrow then I'll tell you everything. And I don't want anything to eat or drink. I just want to get to bed. Please!'

Once in the safety of her own room Laurie had expected the pent-up tears to flow, but she was dry-eyed when she finally got to bed. Her mind was a mass of jumbled thoughts and she knew sleep was out of the question. She had been so right calling Nick infantile—he was a clever man with the instincts of a wilful child. It was her own fault for being hurt now—she had fallen in love with a beautiful image that had no substance, just as she had done many years before in Florence, and with the same outcome.

She turned on her other side, determined to put Nick out of her mind. Slowly, a darker, graver image took his place. Ross, who that

166

evening had called her by her first name for the first time. She knew it was probably a slip of the tongue, not meant to be taken as significant, but nevertheless the recollection was heartwarming, and she needed some fellow-feeling at this time.

*   *   *

She was in a more composed state when she woke up the next morning. She had not lain awake all night after all. Somewhere around midnight she must have fallen asleep, and she hadn't even heard Shirley come to bed.

Her blouse and skirt were still on the chair where she had flung them the previous night. Now she shook them out ready to put away— and then noticed the rose Nick had sent her was still fixed to her blouse. She unpinned it and stared at it as it lay in her palm. It had wilted. It was only a transient thing after all, and perhaps that in itself was symbolic. She hesitated a minute, then dropped it into the waste-paper basket.

She didn't see Nick at all that day. She was busy in the surgery all morning, then she went with Dr Russett to visit the branch surgeries in the Wingfields in the afternoon. When they returned to Merton she was asked to do evening surgery too. Knowing it was Nick's turn on duty she steeled herself for the encounter, but it was Ross who came striding in.

'I—I expected Dr Lawrence,' she said lamely. She knew she had been standing in an expecting attitude.

'He's gone. He left Merton very early this morning.' Ross's manner was brisk. 'I didn't think you wanted to see him again.'

'And you just sent him packing like that—without a word of warning!'

'He got his word of warning all right. He won't bother you again.'

Laurie didn't know whether to laugh or cry. The effrontery, the arrogance of the man—and last night she had felt almost tender towards him! All that vanished in a twinkling; her eyes blazed and she gripped the edge of the desk as a help to contain her temper.

'Look, you weren't doing me any favours sending Nick off. I don't need your help—I can fight my own battles. I don't want anybody running my life for me. I was upset last night, I wasn't in a fit state to work things out with Nick, but I wanted to see him again. I didn't want us to part the way we did; looking back on it now it was all so melodramatic. Neither of us was in our right minds; he was high on drink, I was high on excitement. I wanted us to part like two balanced, civilised beings—but now you've prevented that!'

Ross gave her a long, steady look. 'Did you really want it to come to a parting?' he asked meaningly.

She was about to snap, 'Yes, I did,' but

168

stopped herself.

To be honest, the hope had persisted that Nick might have a change of heart—even give up the idea of going to New York. She didn't know how she would have reacted to that. Now Ross had prevented her from finding out.

He reached for his appointment book, very much the professional man once more, not the Ross who had driven her home in the rain. 'I thought I was doing the right thing,' he said drily. 'But I never seem able to where you're concerned. Perhaps I ill-timed my rescue attempt even—'

'Rescue attempt?' she repeated sharply, then enlightenment dawned and with it a rush of colour to her cheeks. 'Do you mean it wasn't chance your coming along—that you'd *planned* it?'

He smiled faintly. 'What other reason would I have for being near the Blue Cedar? I knew you were expecting an offer of marriage, I heard you tell Shirley so—I also knew Nick wasn't the marrying type. So I thought—I just thought—' he shrugged his shoulders. 'Well, there it is.'

Laurie glared at him. 'And I suppose you think I ought to feel grateful!'

He returned her angry look with one of complete blandness. 'You are under no obligation to me whatsoever. If you think I interfered I'm sorry.' He looked past her at the clock on the wall. 'And now I think it's time we saw to the first patient.'

Laurie walked off with her cheeks burning and the conviction that Ross Cramond was still the most insufferable man she had ever met—yet for the rest of the evening the thought niggled that he had acted out of charity, not the desire to humiliate her. But in her present mood she had no wish to be beholden to any man.

The following morning she received a parcel, and recognising Nick's writing took it to her room to open. He had returned her evening bag and with it was a letter. Her fingers shook as she tore it open.

'Dear Laurie', [he had written—(no more Little Tree, she had cured him of that!)]

'I'm not going to say I'm sorry because it wouldn't be true, but I am sorry for the way we parted. I have many faults, but hypocrisy is not one of them. If I could have got you into bed last night I would have done so and gladly. The only thing I do regret is the misunderstanding which arose between us. I thought you knew I wasn't permanently at Merton surgery, I've always been looking out for something better, though I never dreamed I would land a plum job in the States. And I *am* sorry if I ever gave you the impression I wanted to marry you. I don't intend to get married for years, perhaps never—I value my freedom too much. Ross sent me off with a flea in my ear, but on reflection it's just as well. Things might have been a bit awkward between us, and this extra month will give me the chance to re-kit myself before leaving. Don't begrudge me my future prospects, dear Laurie, as I don't begrudge you a future happiness with the right man. You're a grand girl, and I shall never forget you.

Yours, Nick.

Laurie's first impulse was to screw the letter up and fling it across the room, but on second thoughts she folded it carefully and put it away. She would take it out and read it whenever any lingering regrets over Nick came to torment her, for in many ways it was a cruel letter and wrote *finis* to their relationship in no uncertain way. Perhaps that was what Nick intended. All the same, the hurt persisted, and in spite of her attempt to stem them her tears welled up. She sniffed and brushed them angrily away, and it was then she caught sight of Ross coming back from taking Fergus for his early morning walk.

She leant on the windowsill looking across at him. He was wearing a rough tweed jacket over a pair of tatty old jeans—he was always dressed so impeccably at the surgery that it was difficult to think of him as the same man. Just then a gust of wind lifted his hair, blowing it across his forehead and reinforcing the image of a casual, easygoing man.

171

It came to Laurie then that she had been wrong in her first impression of Ross Cramond. Oh, he could be very infuriating—but to his credit he could be understanding too. And it was that understanding that had sent him driving down the lane past the Blue Cedar— and how many times had he driven up and down expecting to find her? Just as Nick had been sure she would not hesitate to jump into bed with him, so had Ross been equally sure she would do no sure thing.

Yes, she was grateful to him for that.

CHAPTER NINE

Nick's leaving caused hardly a ripple in the smooth running of the Merton practice. Dr Crowson agreed to stay on until a replacement was appointed, and Laurie found herself the only one to give Nick a second thought. It came as a shock to her then to realise that not only was he not missed, but he had never been greatly liked. It was also a dent to her self-esteem to find that she so quickly recovered from her infatuation. To herself she likened it to a case of toothache only cured by drastic action—in this case extraction—then she had to laugh at the idea of comparing Nick with a nagging tooth. That was proof she was cured if anything was!

She told Shirley about the fiasco at the Blue Cedar, finding that the recounting acted like a kind of expiation. 'I've come to the conclusion that I'm not capable of real love,' she finished on a wry note.

'You'll recognise love when it comes, it's not something that hits you suddenly.' There was an unusual glow in Shirley's large tawny eyes. 'Love is something that can grow and strengthen and take such a hold that you'll know without a doubt that it *is* the real thing.'

Laurie was too surprised to answer. She had never encountered this mood before. Shirley could be high-spirited, tender, lovable, noisy and even huffy at time. But *romantic*—this was something new. Laurie wondered if a man was the cause, and if so who was he? She had been so wrapped up in herself lately she had hardly been aware of any change in Shirley. She hoped whoever the man was he was good enough for her.

The morning Mr Burge came to the surgery for the results of his blood test brought home to Laurie that it was exactly a week ago since Nick had left—and for three days of that week she had been too busy to give him a thought. There was a moral there somewhere. She ushered Mr Burge in to see Ross and then went off to Dispensary to re-stock the travelling bag ready for the doctor's visit to the branch surgeries that afternoon. She was still in with Shirley when Mr Burge tapped on the counter.

He handed in the prescription Dr Ross had written out. 'Well, ladies,' he beamed at them, 'the doctor has given me a clean bill of health, said my potassium level is a bit low but nothing to worry about. He's prescribed me some quinine tablets for my cramp—quinine, I ask you!' Later when Shirley had given him the bottle of shiny white capsules, he held it up to the light, stared, and shook his head. 'Just look at the little beauties—what wouldn't we have given for some of 'em in Burma in 'forty-three? Watched my pals dying of malaria for the want of quinine, and the MO tearing his hair out from frustration. Now I've been given them just for cramp. It's a rum old world.'

'As long as they cure your cramp,' said Laurie.

He grinned at her. 'You're right, Nurse, I've got no cause to complain. Did you like them peaches? You come and see me again, I've got a consignment of them pink grapefruit just in. Half-price to you and your friend here.'

That evening Shirley suggested a walk round the square before bed. Laurie was reluctant to leave the fire, but Shirley seemed restless, and when Shirley was restless it was easier to contain her out of doors than in.

The square was deserted, nobody else was braving the cold. The stars looked very near and were exceptionally bright, a sign of frost. 'Just look at that,' said Shirley, pointing to a shop window stuck about with bits of cottonwool to represent snow. 'They've started to decorate for Christmas already and it isn't even November yet. Next thing, we'll be told how many shopping days there are left!'

'I'm not worrying about Christmas yet,' said Laurie. 'My exam comes first.'

'When's that?'

'In a month's time. And I haven't even started any revision yet. I must get down to it.'

They passed a fried fish shop, and Shirley sniffed. 'Oh, doesn't that just tickle the nose? I'm starving, Laurie—it's this cold wind. Shall we get a bag of chips each for supper?'

'I might have known this walk wasn't just for exercise—that there was a method in your madness. And I bet you haven't even got any money with you!'

'Cross my heart I haven't. But you have, you always keep some loose change in your pocket. Provident girl!'

Armed with a bag each, they retraced their steps to the Green. The chips were warm in their fingers, the smell enticing. Shirley was the first to succumb, but presently they were both dipping in and laughing. Life is good, thought Laurie fleetingly. It's the little things that make it worthwhile—like friendship and a good laugh. She was feeling sentimental.

Then as they rounded a corner they walked into two men with a dog. It was Ross with a short stocky man whom Laurie recognised as Howard Saunders, a local dentist—and Fergus, of course. Laurie was glad to see he was on a lead. Mr Saunders was wearing a hat, and he doffed it as he recognised the girls. Ross said jokingly, 'Alfresco supper—and very nice too. May I?' and he helped himself to a chip from Shirley's bag.

In the light of the street lamp Laurie saw that Shirley had turned a deep crimson. She was also too confused to speak, hampered too by the fact that her mouth was full, but as the girls walked on Laurie wondered about that blush. Shirley wasn't embarrassed being caught eating chips in the street—she couldn't have cared less. Why, then? Walking into Ross unawares? Did he have that effect on her? All these questions Laurie felt worrying, hoping that Shirley of all people hadn't fallen a victim to Ross's obscure charms. What was it about him, that he could attract such dissimilar women as Louise Fellowes and Marcia Peacock, and now—heaven forbid—Shirley? Laurie's former mood of cheerfulness passed and Shirley too fell silent. It was a sober pair who turned in at the gate of the cottage.

*　　　*　　　*

The cold snap didn't last for long. At the end of October the days were as warm as June, and it was getting dark now by six o'clock. Laurie noticed in her drives through the lanes how the landscape was changing colour. The beech

176

trees had turned from gold to russet and the leaves of the maples were a brilliant crimson. The creeper on the walls of Sinclair House was like a mural of golds and reds and browns, and everywhere were berries. Migrant birds like fieldfares and redwings were busy in the hedgerows just as native birds like thrushes and blackbirds were plundering the gardens. It was a time of mellowness and reflection—it was also a time for her to get on with some serious studying. She was already ticking the days off on the calendar. She now had the date of her exam, it was during the last week of November, and she told Dr Russett as arrangements had to be made for her to have time off for the trip to London. Dr Russett promised to have a word with Ross about it.

And then there was a newcomer to the cottage—a tiny bundle of black and white fur with eyes as brilliant as emeralds and a coat like plush. A patient had found her in her garden and had told Shirley that as nobody had come to claim her, the kitten would have to make a visit to the vet's.

'I told her it was sheer emotional blackmail,' said Shirley as she deposited the kitten in Laurie's lap. 'But how could I refuse to take her—isn't she cute? She's already been dubbed Kitty, but we'll have to think up something more original.'

But they didn't, because she only answered to the name of Kitty, quickly displaying a disposition that was not to be put upon. Just as quickly she took complete charge of them, and after that their time was never their own.

Kitty was keeping Laurie company one afternoon while Laurie finished off the week's ironing. It was her afternoon off, and there was an open textbook on the table with a notepad beside it, but Laurie's eyes ached from reading and ironing wasn't quite so taxing, so she had brought the ironing-board into the sitting-room and propped open the front door so that she could hear the robin singing in the front garden. It was a still, mild day and pale sunlight made a small pool of light on the floor which Kitty was constantly attacking, thinking it something alive.

Suddenly the door crashed further open and Fergus sprang into the room, dragging Shirley behind him at the other end of his lead.

Laurie backed away. 'Why did you bring that brute in here?' she demanded furiously.

'I didn't bring him—he brought me. Rather, it was a two-way affair.' Shirley unwound the lead from her right wrist and dropped it. In the meantime Fergus had spotted the kitten and froze, looking as if he had turned to stone.

'I'm not staying,' said Shirley, making for the stairs. 'I'm really on my way to Sinclair House to take Fergus home. Ross called in at the surgery with him—he was in the middle of taking him for a walk and wanted something he'd left behind, when a phone call came for him. Gosh, you should have been there, there was an instant flap! Ross asked me to take Fergus home, and you know how the silly old thing always gets excited when he sees me—he jumped up and tore a lump out of my tights. I must change them.'

'What was the phone call about?' asked Laurie.

'I haven't an earthly. Ross yelled at me to take Fergus and went tearing off. Will he be all right with you while I pop upstairs?'

'He certainly won't—he might savage Kitty!'

Shirley looked over her shoulder, then burst into laughter.

'Who's savaging who?' she said, chortling.

Kitty had transferred her attention from the patch of sunlight to the loop of Fergus's lead, quite unaware of the 'brute' attached to the other end. *He* crouched as still as a statue, only his eyes moving, and giving plaintive whimpers. Suddenly Kitty noticed him. She arched her back and spat, then did a crab-like dance towards him. Fergus dived for cover under the table.

Uncontrolled tears poured down Shirley's cheeks. 'I don't believe it—I just don't believe it! I wish Ross could see this. Fergus!—come out from there, you great coward!'

Fergus crawled into sight again, flat on his belly and his eyes liquid with self-pity. Giving Kitty as wide a berth as possible, he dashed for the door, but Kitty, who had decided that he was more of a plaything than a menace, pounced on his tail and hung there; Shirley swore afterwards that she actually grinned. Fergus gave a howl of anguish and rolled over on his back in surrender, and Kitty immediately landed on his chest and purring blissfully began to knead his fur.

By this time Laurie was also helpless with laughter. 'And to think I was scared of that old fraud!' she said, wiping her tears away. '"Fergus the Teeth", I don't think—"Fergus the Timid", more like it. Fancy a great dog like that being scared of such a tiny kitten!'

'I think it's rather touching,' said Shirley. 'He could squash Kitty with one paw if he wanted to. He's just frightened of his own strength, that's what—just like his master.'

Nothing could have sobered Laurie up more quickly than the manner of Shirley's reference to Ross. 'What's the matter?' asked Shirley, seeing her change of expression.

'I can't help noticing lately how you bring Ross's name into our conversation at the slightest excuse. I hope—oh, Shirley, I don't want to see you smitten too—'

Shirley stared. 'What on earth are you on about?'

'I'm talking about you and Ross, of course. Do you think I haven't noticed—well, the way you feel?'

Shirley's expression was an odd mixture of confusion and archness. 'Do I reveal my

180

feelings so much? And I thought I was being so clever! You're right, pet, about the way I feel, but not for Ross—it's Howard Saunders.'

Howard Saunders the dentist! Laurie was bereft of speech. But he was middle-aged—well, anyway, in his forties at least—and a widower besides, with a son of fourteen. And he was shorter than Shirley and not even good-looking. But he did have a pleasant voice and a very courteous manner, and the kindest eyes she'd ever seen—and Shirley loved him. That was plain.

'Why didn't you tell me?' she moaned. 'Letting me make a fool of myself like that!'

'We're not telling anybody—not until the Christmas holidays, when Robert, that's Howard's son, comes home from school and then we can talk about it openly. We want Robert to be the first to know, it's only fair. Oh, Shirley, I'm so happy!'

Laurie dimpled, but somewhat wryly. 'And to think of all that sympathy I wasted on you—you and your frequent visits to the dentist! I suppose that was the only way you two could be together without causing gossip. Does Ross know?'

'Yes, he had to know; he's Howard's closest friend. Now I must change my tights. There'll be a queue at the dispensary from here to kingdom come if I don't get a move on!'

For the first time in weeks Laurie's mind went back to Nick. She remembered Shirley's

words when they had last talked about him—
'You'll recognise it when it comes, it's not
something that hits you suddenly. Love is
something that can grow and strengthen and
take such a hold that you'll know without a
doubt that it's real.' Her own attachment to
Nick had not held because there had been
nothing to hold on to, no sure foundation. She
sighed, then smiled as she heard Shirley
whistling overhead. Her happiness was
infectious.

The two animals had settled their
differences. Fergus was lying on his side with
Kitty curled up against his flank. Laurie knelt
down beside them.

'You lovable old impostor,' she told Fergus.
'Trying to make out you were fierce and scaring
the daylights out of me! Do you know what you
are—all bark and no bite!' She bent and kissed
the top of his head, and his tail thudded on the
floor in response. Laurie sat back on her heels
and considered him. All bark and no bite, yes—
that described him admirably. Fleetingly she
wondered whether it might also describe his
master.

Later that afternoon when she had settled
down once more to her books Julie phoned to
say she was wanted at the surgery immediately.
There was such an urgency about Julie's voice
that Laurie didn't bother to change but ran
across as she was in jeans and old shirt with her
hair tied back with a piece of black tape.

She had been told to go to Dr Russett's room, and was surprised to find Ross also there; she had an idea by what Shirley had said that he was out on a visit. He was pacing the room, his hands thrust characteristically in his pockets, his brows lowered.

He seemed not to notice Laurie, he was too taken up with thundering at Dr Russett. 'What was I thinking of?' he demanded of her. 'There were all the classic symptoms, plain for me to see, and yet I missed them. Loss of weight, no stamina, anxiety, sleeplessness—I should have realised. I had my doubts at times; I wasn't all that certain it was a straightforward case of anorexia nervosa—was I?' he suddenly barked at Laurie, making her jump. She didn't know yet what he was storming on about, but guessed it had something to do with Louise Fellowes.

'We all jumped to the same conclusion,' said Dr Russett placatingly. 'We all thought—'

'Thought—thought! Doctors shouldn't *think*—they should know. Louise may pay for my stupid mistake with her life. Well, I must get back to the hospital.' He looked at Laurie with anxious eyes, red-rimmed with fatigue. 'I want you to follow me. Louise particularly asked for you. Dr Russett will fill you in,' and then he was gone, like a power-house of energy suddenly released.

'Sit down a moment, Laurie.' Dr Russett also looked tired. She rubbed her eyes. 'Colonel Fellowes found Louise unconscious earlier on today. I do wish he'd called us in before, but he didn't even worry at first. He said Louise often has fainting fits, he put it down to the fact that she didn't eat enough, and I have a feeling he wasn't all that sympathetic. Louise's mother died when she was still at school and she hasn't had many home comforts, you might say. Ross went over straight away and found her in a diabetic coma. He wanted to have her taken to the District Hospital, but the Colonel insisted she should go to the Cottage Hospital—he's on the Hospital Committee and feels he has a proprietary claim. Louise is out of her coma now, but it was touch and go.' Again Dr Russett rubbed her eyes. 'She's suffering from diabetes mellitus, not anorexia nervosa as we all thought. It's so easy to jump to conclusions, and I was chiefly to blame. We all knew she was hopelessly in love with Robin Shipley of Merton Hall—I assumed that was the reason for her condition, fretting her heart out over a married man. And all the time the poor girl was suffering from diabetes!'

Laurie was glad she was sitting down; at that moment her legs might not have supported her. 'I thought it was Dr Ross she was in love with,' she said lamely.

Dr Russett looked startled. 'What gave you that idea?'

'I don't really know. The way she behaved with him, I think.'

184

The other woman nodded. 'Yes, I can see how Louise gives that impression—she does idolise Ross, but only in the role of a big brother. Ross has always found time for her since she was a small child. He helped her with her homework and taught her to ride a bike— things that her father should have been doing really. She repaid him by following him about like a little shadow until the Honourable Robin came on the scene. He inherited the estate when Louise was about sixteen or seventeen— an impressionable age. He went abroad for several years and when he returned he was married. He didn't notice Louise had turned into a young woman in the meantime. He even went on calling her Podge, which was a childhood nickname. Very tactless, considering his wife was so fashionably thin. That was when Louise first started to diet and put us on the wrong track. It's too easy to jump to conclusions—we fool ourselves all the time.'

Words that Laurie was to recall many times in the course of the next few days. Louise was now out of danger, but needed constant supervision. Ross had obtained Matron's grudging consent for Laurie to nurse the sick girl, and Laurie spent a good deal of her time in the private ward. After a few days Louise recovered sufficiently for the intravenous drip to be discontinued, and her unhealthy pallor slowly gave way to a more natural colour. Her eyes were still those of a very sick patient, hollow-looking and dull. She liked Laurie to be there whenever she awakened from her fitful sleep, as if fearful of being on her own.

Ross was a frequent visitor, and not only in his professional capacity. Occasionally Colonel Fellowes came, but he was so out of place in a sickroom that it was a relief to all when he left. Once Robin Shipley called, and tactlessly brought his wife with him. She too looked out of place, perched uncomfortably on the edge of her chair as if ready to escape at any minute, looking beautiful but saying nothing. Robin had a pleasant way with him and was extremely civil, but that being said, Laurie could see nothing else in his favour, and she wondered how Louise could have been so impossibly attracted to him. She could not help comparing him with Ross, who could have made two of Robin both in size and personality. But his visit had one unexpected outcome: from that time Louise began steadily to mend. It was if she had come to terms with her insuperable position and realised that her destiny depended entirely on herself and that a sick body was no help to a broken heart.

'I don't like Matron,' she remarked, à propos of nothing, one afternoon a day or two later. She was sitting up for the first time, looking quite attractive in a pink bedjacket that reflected her delicate colouring. 'Do you notice the way she always appears just as Ross arrives? As if she has a private radar set beamed on to him?'

Laurie chuckled. 'You must be getting better, to notice things like that!'

'I've got nothing much else to do, lying here. And did you hear the way she snapped at Debbie (Debbie was the pupil nurse who had first shown Laurie over the hospital) when she came to tell her she was wanted on the phone? It didn't suit Matron to be called away just then, she was about to invite Ross to have tea in her room, I could tell that by the look in her eye. Have you noticed her predatory eyes? She never moves her head, just swivels her eyes around like laser beams.'

This time Laurie laughed outright. It was good to hear someone else saying what she had been thinking for some time—but she mustn't encourage Louise any longer. She walked over to the bed and gently lowered the sick girl into a reclining position. 'You're getting too flushed and you're over-excited and you're talking too much,' she said, her hand on Louise's brow. 'And if you start running a temperature Dr Ross will put the blame on me.'

'I'm worried about Ross,' confessed Louise. 'Have you noticed how tired he begins to look? I'm sure he's overtaxing himself.'

Laurie silently agreed. She had heard from Shirley that he was doing the branch surgeries single-handed, not liking to impose on Dr Crowson and refusing to let Rusty help out as she had taken on the evening clinics. She

187

couldn't help thinking of Nick then, wondering if he ever compared the country practice he had turned his back on with the fashionable clinic in New York. No, she didn't suppose he ever gave them a thought, and the idea didn't hurt any more. Nick Lawrence and Robin Shipley had a lot in common, and perhaps that was what had brought such instant rapport between Louise and herself. Had Ross suspected that? And was that why he insisted that she and she alone should nurse Louise? A faint smile curved her lips. He was a deep one!

One morning that week she called in at the surgery on her way to the hospital. It was just over two weeks before she was due to re-sit her exam and she was using any spare time at the hospital doing revision. She had left an anatomy book in the treatment room which she wanted to collect. Ross was standing with his back to her, helping himself to some dressings.

He called out. 'Come in—you won't disturb me. I'm just stocking up before going on to Lynch Green.' Laurie wondered if he could see through the back of his head if he had recognised her footsteps. He turned slowly, and the look he gave her was both quizzical and challenging.

'I heard you've made another conquest.'

'Oh?' Wild thoughts raced through her head. Who could he have in mind?'

'Yes. Shirley told me you have Fergus eating out of your hand. What love potion did you use?'

She laughed. When he was in this mood she felt quite at ease with him. 'Oh, no magic drug—it was all Kitty's doing. She showed him up for the soft-hearted old sham he is.'

A sardonic look crossed Ross's lean face. 'That's quite a common story—a beast being tamed by a mere scrap of femininity.' Was it her imagination, or was there a hidden meaning in his words? To her annoyance she found herself blushing and was conscious of him watching her as she crossed to pick up her book. His eyes went to it.

'Ah yes, that reminds me—Dr Russett mentioned your exam and said you wanted some time off at the end of November. I suggest you take a whole week—you deserve a break after the hours you've put in nursing Louise. How do you feel about your exam?'

'More confident than I did last time,' Laurie told him.

'That's a good sign. As long as you don't drop a tray of instruments and lose your nerve like you did before, you should have nothing to worry about.'

It was not the most tactful thing he could have said in the circumstances, and Laurie felt all her old antipathy towards him rushing back. He was too arrogant to realise that it was his attitude, the way he had stared at her, that had made her lose her nerve. Dropping the instrument tray had only been a contributory factor.

With a self-control she was surprised she possessed she lifted her chin and returned his infuriating smile with a frigid glare.

'You needn't worry on that score, Dr Ross,' she said steadily. 'I have my nerves under perfect control now. I've had plenty of practice since working here!'

CHAPTER TEN

Ten days after being taken to hospital Louise had recovered sufficiently to think about leaving. Though this remarkable recovery was chiefly due to Ross's skill and Laurie's careful nursing, it also owed something to the fact that Louise herself was determined to come to grips with her condition.

It had been arranged that she was to spend a few weeks convalescing with some cousins on her mother's side. Once before, as a girl of thirteen, she had fled to them during a different crisis in her life—the death of her mother. Cathy and Frank Foster were then newly married and managing a stud farm in Dorset. They had come far since then, now owning the farm and an adjoining riding school. From Louise's point of view it was the perfect setting in which to recuperate.

Ross had offered to drive her there, and the

Fosters had at once insisted that he stayed on for a few days. At first he had been reluctant to take up their offer, then Laurie overheard Dr Russett going for him.

'A sick doctor is no use to himself or to his patients,' she declared. 'This is just the break that you need, and you'd be a fool to turn it down.' At times Rusty surprised them by her imperious manner—on this occasion it paid off.

On the day they were leaving Laurie went to the hospital to help Louise pack. She found her in an excited, restless mood, not able to keep still, constantly going to the window to see if Ross was coming.

'He came in to see me last night and had a heart-to-heart with me,' she told Laurie. 'He went over the same ground regarding my diabetes and said that the insulin had now stabilised it. He said he was only discharging me because he was satisfied I'd mastered the technique of injecting myself. I said that was entirely due to you and how patient you were with me, because I was so stupidly squeamish at first. He wanted to check that I had enough insulin to last while I'm away.'

Laurie showed her a small case. 'Everything you require is in here—syringes and ampoules. I've packed a month's supply, so that should see you through, but if the unforeseen happens and you run short contact the local GP immediately.'

There was a crunch of tyres on the forecourt outside, and Louise jumped up from the bed. 'That's Ross, bless him—now we can be off.' There were two hectic spots of colour on her cheeks which gave Laurie cause for concern. It would be ironic if Louise should start running a temperature now—then she realised that it wasn't a temperature but the delight at seeing Ross that gave Louise such a colour, and she felt even more disturbed without knowing why, except to think how unfortunate if Louise were to fall in love with Ross on the rebound. But unfortunate for whom? She couldn't answer that.

Laurie stood on the hospital steps beside Matron and waved Louise and Ross away. When the car had finally disappeared Matron relaxed her fixed smile and with a muttered, 'Well, now that Miss Pampered has gone, perhaps we can get on with some real work!' she flounced off. But Laurie stayed on for a moment or two, remembering Ross's firm handshake and the searching look he had given her with his last words of advice. 'Take the rest of the day off. Get out into the fresh air; you've been cooped up in this hospital far too long. You know what Rusty said about sick doctors? That goes for sick nurses too.'

His unusual concern made her confused, not knowing how to answer. She felt a sudden lightheartedness that only lasted until she saw with what tenderness and care he settled

Louise on the back seat of his car. She recalled Rusty telling her that the only women Ross was interested in were sick women. Whether it was that or whether he was responding to Louise's obvious attraction to him, either way it left Laurie feeling disturbed.

But she took his advice, and changed into some old clothes with the intention of going for a walk over the hills. She only got as far as the market square. It was market day and the crowded stalls were stocked with produce of all kinds, many of them with Christmas goods on offer. Laurie couldn't resist the allure of a bargain, and she loved to hear the lively patter of the stallholders as they held up 'unrepeatable offers' for inspection. She was laughing at the antics of the man in charge of the china stall when she felt a touch on her arm and turned.

'Nurse—Nurse Bush!'

At first she didn't recognise the young woman who had spoken, then with a start of surprise saw that it was Lucy Wilson, but what a different Lucy! She had let her hair grow out to its natural brown shade and had discarded the bizarre make-up which had made her look so odd. It was as if she no longer needed such gimmicks to hide behind. She looked fitter too, and was delighted to see Laurie.

Laurie returned her smile. 'Mrs Wilson, I *am* glad to see you. It's been on my conscience not coming to see you as I promised, but I've been rather tied up with a patient lately. How is Timmy now?'

'He's fine. Full of mischief still—that ducking didn't dampen his spirits any. Mrs Lomax is looking after him today to give me a chance to do some shopping. The neighbours have been ever so good to me since all that fuss about Timmy. It's not their fault they weren't before—they offered, but I was always too touchy,' Lucy conceded with a grimace. 'Things are a lot better for me now, Nurse. A lot of good came from all the publicity. We were on the local telly, did you know? I don't know whether it was that that made my landlord ashamed of the state of our cottage or whether the conservationists got on to him, but he's had a complete change of heart and now the cottage is being done up and modernised. I won't know where I am, with hot water laid on and a bathroom!' She grinned girlishly. 'I meant to write and tell you how much Timmy appreciated that book you sent him. The little imp thinks it was written especially for him. He's learnt it off by heart, the number of times he's made me read it to him—now he pretends he can read it himself. He keeps asking when are you coming to see him.'

'Just as soon as I can—you tell him that.'

Laurie walked away with an inward glow of satisfaction. It had been a good day from a nurse's point of view—first Louise on the way to recovery and now Lucy Wilson and Timmy

194

happily settled. It wasn't entirely her doing, she was only a cog in the wheel, but she didn't think anyone would begrudge her believing not an unimportant cog.

She marvelled to think how speedily she had fitted into the practice, especially when remembering that first disastrous day when she had been ready to catch the next train home to Woodford. It was hard to believe now how much she depended on the friendship of Shirley and Dr Russett—and yes, she would have to admit it—Ross too. In some ways he more than the others, for he was the king-pin of the practice and set the tone for its reputation of efficiency and good organisation. Her infatuation for Nick had blinded her to Ross's good points. She had seen only his arrogance and his pride—and that too could have been her own fault; her ill-feeling towards him reflected back upon her.

She sighed. The thought of ever leaving the practice gave her a pang. It was a possibility she hated to think of, but unless she passed her exam this time, she knew there was no alternative. Ross wasn't the kind of man to go back on his word. All thoughts of loitering round the market suddenly left her; she could make use of this free time to do more studying. She turned up the collar of her jacket against the wind and hurried back to the cottage.

The next day she plunged back into the old routine, caught up in a maelstrom of autumnal coughs and chills. Ross's absence became more marked as it was brought home upon her how much the others relied upon his judgment. More than once she overheard such phrases as; 'Better hold that over and let Dr Ross decide,' and 'Ross will know what to do about this query. Is it urgent, can it wait a few days?' There was even discontent among some of the patients who refused to see anybody else but Dr Ross. One old man complained, 'But I always have a bottle of medicine for my bronchitis. Dr Ross gives me something his father used to make up. I don't want that ole rubbish!' This to Shirley, who was trying to give him some anti-congestion tablets.

Hearing Ross's name so often from patients and staff alike Laurie told herself it was small wonder she couldn't get him out of her mind. She knew she would be pleased to see him again, but she believed that was because she had the matter of her leave to arrange. She had decided not to take a whole week off to go to London, she could be ill spared at the present. Three days would be ample, and that would give her a clear day for the exam.

There was no surgery on Saturday mornings, though a doctor was always on call and an emergency system in operation. Laurie had got behind with her secretarial work and there was little peace in the cottage when Shirley had time on her hands, so this Saturday Laurie took herself off to the surgery to work in absolute quiet.

She was sitting in Reception bringing the record cards up to date when she heard the outer door open. Always on the alert because of the drugs on the premises, she turned quickly and saw Ross. Her heart began to thud in an aggravating way, but she told herself it was only the unexpectedness of his appearance.

'Y-you weren't expected back until Monday.'

'I know—that's what was arranged.' He seemed slightly embarrassed himself. 'I guessed you'd be busy, then when I phoned Rusty yesterday to see how things were she sounded so weary I decided to come straight back. I arrived too late last night to look in then. I've come over to see if you've cooked up anything for me on Monday.' He slipped the appointments book from under her elbow and leafed through it.

A sense of well-being came over Laurie. All problems would slot into place now, all nuisances be ironed out. Stealing a secret look at him, she thought, He looks so cheerful, then—I wonder if it was being with Louise.

He caught her eye. 'Anything up? You look anxious.'

Confused, she answered his question with another. 'How is Louise?'

He seated himself on the edge of the desk before speaking. 'Even two days in Dorset has made a heck of a change in her—a change for the better, I hasten to add. The Fosters are a nice young couple, and there's a brother—a David Foster, the local vet, who spends a lot of time at the farm. At least he does now—whether he did so before Louise arrived I wouldn't know.' He laughed quietly, then said in a more serious tone, 'He'll be good for Louise, help her through this sticky patch—'

Laurie hardly heard his last sentence, her mind was too concentrated on this sudden David Foster. It was wonderful to think that Louise had met someone who might help her forget Robin Shipley completely. She didn't see anything inconsistent in that idea, considering her previous concern that Louise might fall for Ross on the rebound. Now she welcomed the idea that Louise could fall for this David instead, though she did have the uncomfortable conviction that somewhere in all this her own personal feelings had become involved.

Ross said with some vehemence, 'I never could understand why Louise fell for Robin—or why she didn't transfer her affections to Nick Lawrence when he came on the scene. Most women made fools of themselves over Nick—but somehow Louise avoided that.'

The minute he uttered them he realised the enormity of his unfortunate words. He sprang to his feet, but Laurie was quicker—she had reached the door before he caught her. She tried to resist him, beating him off with her fists, her face red with mortification. 'Oh, how could you!' she sobbed.

His grip on her shoulders was like a band of steel, his eyes went dark with remorse. 'Look, I didn't mean it that way. I wasn't getting at you. God knows what made me say such a thing.' He stared at her, seeing her eyes slowly fill with tears that emphasised their startling blueness. 'I didn't realise you still cared. I'm sorry for being such a blundering fool.' His hands dropped to his sides and his voice went thin.

Impatiently Laurie brushed her tears away. She wanted to say, It's not what you think. I'm not crying for Nick, he doesn't mean anything to me any more. It's you—seeing you again so unexpectedly and knowing how much I've missed you. And knowing too that it's hopeless to feel like this, that I'm just—I'm just another member of the staff. How can I say all this aloud? How can I describe this strange mixture of pain and pleasure whenever I'm with you? You'd only be embarrassed, or worse still, laugh at me.

She was hardly aware that Ross had left. She turned blindly back to her work, in no state to think coherently. In the end she gave up. She would leave it now until Monday.

But there was to be no work at the surgery on Monday, for on Sunday morning when she came down late from bed, Shirley having gone out early to meet Howard, Laurie found Kitty chasing a folded sheet of paper along the floor. Listlessly she picked it up, then saw it was a note addressed to herself. Her heart gave a telltale lurch as she recognised Ross's writing.

'I see there's nothing booked for me on Monday,' he had written. 'How would you like to take the day off and come with me to Cheltenham? It's not a question of skiving, it's a bona fide professional visit, though mixed with pleasure. If you agree to come with me I know I've been forgiven for my stupid remark of yesterday, and I'll pick you up at ten o'clock.'

Laurie read the note twice more before folding it and putting it in the pocket of her dressing-gown. Then with a secret smile she swooped on Kitty and planted a kiss on the top of her silky head. As far as Kitty was concerned this was an open invitation to a saucer of milk, and she miaowed her protests when she was plonked on the floor again, and the giver of benefices disappeared up the stairs in a flutter of skirts.

Ross must have slipped the note through the door after Shirley had left, otherwise it would have been brought up to her, Laurie thought. She giggled. What a torment of curiosity Shirley had escaped, wondering why Ross should send a secret note to Laurie on a Sunday morning!

There was a sharp frost that night, but the morning dawned clear with a promise of a fine day to follow. Laurie was up before it was light. Through the bare trees across the Green she could see lights on in Ross's flat, so he was up early too. She had given a lot of thought as to what to wear—something serviceable but at the same time a little special, not that she had a large wardrobe to choose from. There was the new lambswool sweater and grey tweed skirt she had bought to wear to London. The sweater was the colour of cornflowers. 'You should always wear that colour,' Shirley had said when she tried it on. 'It matches your eyes.' It was a pity she would have to cover it up with her old raincoat, though if the sun came out she might get away with carrying it over her arm instead. She brushed out her hair until it crackled, then fluffed it out with her hands, and it ballooned out on to her shoulders from a centre parting, gleaming blue-black in the faint morning light.

Ross called for her promptly at ten and once they had left Merton and were bowling along the highway in a westerly direction he told her the reason for this trip. He asked her whether she had heard about the Andersons, Mrs Anderson had been his father's housekeeper and her husband the gardener, and Laurie vaguely recalled Dr Russett mentioning them her first day at Merton.

'They lived in the top flat at Sinclair House?' she ventured.

'That's right—until last year, then they went off to this little cottage near Cheltenham. Mr Anderson had a hip replacement operation a week ago, he's still in hospital, and I'd like to see for myself how he's progressing. I phoned through to the Sister of the ward yesterday asking her to let Mrs Anderson know we'd be coming today. Unfortunately she isn't on the phone, and now telegrams have been done away with it's a puzzle to know how to get a message through sometimes. I didn't want to catch Andy unawares.'

'Andy? You call her that?'

'Not to her face, she's far too prim and proper—but don't get me wrong, she's a treasure. She was a kind of nanny to me for years.'

He lapsed into a comfortable silence and Laurie took the opportunity to watch the scudding countryside. Though she had been working in the Cotswolds for three months she was only familiar with the triangle that made up Merton, Lynch Green and the Wingfields. This was new territory, just as charming and a delight to the eye in spite of its late autumnal appearance. The greens and yellows had deepened into russets and bronze and the sheep-hugging hills were misted over with patches of vapour. Most of the trees were bare, though the beeches still clung tenaciously to leaves like crinkled brown paper.

Ross broke into her thoughts. 'We're in no hurry, so I thought I'd show you some parts of the Cotswolds you haven't seen before. Do you know Broadway? We could have coffee there. I like it best out of season when the tourists have left. It's a lovely old place, in spite of the souvenir shops.' He drove on to the next crossroads and turned right, then after a brief detour through lanes, they were on another main road. Laurie saw the signpost to Broadway.

They had been climbing steadily for some miles, and presently she saw what looked like the ruins of a castle on the brow of a hill and pointed it out. Ross shook his head. 'No, not a mediaeval castle, but an eighteenth-century folly. It's a famous landmark.'

He pulled off the road into a grassy turning. 'We can park here, it's a good spot for seeing the view.' Except for the sheep they had the place to themselves. Ross took her by her elbow to help her over the uneven ground. Here it was so high the wind caught her hair, sweeping it into her eyes. She parted it with both hands laughing. Ross pointed out the land dropping away into the Vale of Evesham, a counterpane of muted colours and misty distances. She could feel his love for this countryside like a tangible thing, he was proud to be sharing it with her, and stealing a look at him she detected a tranquillity she would never have suspected he possessed.

'On a clear day it's possible to see the Black Mountains of Wales from here,' he remarked, then added reflectively, 'I must bring you back here in the spring. To see the Vale of Evesham in blossom time is an unforgettable sight.'

He took her back to the car. 'And now we'll cruise down Fish Hill into Broadway. The hill's not all that steep—one in ten—but it curves and swoops and falls for a long, long way.' He didn't speak again until they were descending, the car purring along without effort even in low gear. 'I cycled down here once,' he said. 'I took my feet off the pedals and just took off. I was fourteen at the time and it was the nearest I ever came to flying.'

Laurie gasped. 'Whatever made you do such a thing? A dare?'

Ross went sober. 'No, I was trying to escape from a problem. I wasn't old enough to realise then that problems have a habit of catching up with you.' The laugh he gave was slightly scornful as if he were mocking himself.

'You didn't cycle up again!'

He gave another mirthless laugh. 'I don't remember the return journey. I came up in an ambulance—unconscious. I fell off my bike at the foot of the hill and knocked myself out.'

Laurie didn't like to question him further, there was a grimness about him now that was all too familiar. She wondered about that runaway bike ride—could it have had any connection with the revelation that his mother had not died as he had supposed but had run off with another man? Rusty had once said he had discovered the truth when he was about fourteen. Ross had lapsed into thoughtfulness again, but as he pulled up in front of an hotel

204

that served coffee his former good humour came to the fore. It was as if he was making an effort not to let anything spoil this day.

Laurie could see what he meant about Broadway—it was a jewel of a place, a sprawling village of honey-coloured houses and shops that stretched either side of the main road amidst giant horse-chestnut trees.

They sat in the lounge of the hotel to drink their coffee, looking through a bow window on to the street. Across the road a line of trees stood black against the blue sky, and Ross nodded to them. 'They're a sight to see too in early summer when they're bright with red candles. Whenever I see horse-chestnuts in bloom I'm reminded of Broadway.'

'There were red horse-chestnuts where I lived in Woodford,' Laurie told him.

He smiled at her. 'I refuse to believe that Essex horse-chestnuts are better than Cotswolds horse-chestnuts. You must come here with me next year to see for yourself.'

This was the second time that morning he had alluded to her still being with the practice in a year's time. It gave her the courage to say, 'But I'm only here on approval—on the understanding that I pass my exam. Supposing I don't?'

The look he gave her sent the blood to her cheeks. 'Have you any reason to believe you won't?' he asked quietly.

She shook her head. 'I feel more confident

205

this time.'

Ross gave a faint smile. 'From what I've seen of your work I don't think you need have any fears. And if the worst happens and you do plough your exam, it won't matter. I'm afraid the practice wouldn't be able to function without you, you'll have to stay.'

Laurie looked at him with startled eyes. 'But you were so adamant!'

'And so were you—accusing me of being the cause of your failing your exam before. Shall we start again from scratch? No more accusations.'

She blushed again, this time from discomfort. It was the first time he had referred to that fatal interview on her first day at Merton, and that was something that in her present mood she wanted to forget.

He looked at his watch, then got to his feet in a purposeful manner. 'Come along, no more loitering, I promised to call on Andy about twelve o'clock. I've booked a table for lunch at the Green Dragon, then in the afternoon we'll call at the hospital to see Mr Anderson. I hope that meets with your approval.' He grinned at her, the grin offsetting the slightly mocking words. While he paid the bill Laurie went to the powder room to freshen up. She smoothed her hair and renewed her make-up, staring at her reflection with serious eyes. 'You know what's happening, don't you? You're falling deeply in love with him. Beware! This won't be another Nick Lawrence affair that you'll recover from in a matter of days. This could be real heartbreak. He hasn't given you any encouragement, he's just being pleasantly polite.' She sighed, shutting off such teasing thoughts, wishing she could take things as they came and not become so deeply involved, but that was in her nature.

But she was buoyant again by the time she joined Ross. Like him she was determined not to let anything spoil this day. All the way to Cheltenham he entertained her with stories of his schooldays there. 'It's a gracious town,' he said more than once. 'They knew how to build houses, those Regency architects. Thank the Lord the Cotswolds haven't been spoilt by modern housing. Have you noticed how newly-built houses have to be stone-clad to tone in with the existing properties? Unfortunately the rule doesn't apply to Cheltenham—some parts of it are being murdered.'

They had to branch off before reaching Cheltenham in order to visit Mrs Anderson. Her cottage was in a village five miles to the south. He followed a signpost pointing to East Cantley and told her to look out for a timber-framed cottage with a thatched roof about a mile past a T-junction. In high summer the cottage would have been hidden from the road by trees, but now through the bare branches Laurie suddenly spotted it and called out.

Ross braked hard. 'I always shoot past the

207

damn place,' he said. 'I'll pull in here on to the grass verge—there's no room to park in the garden.' This was true, there was only a narrow brick path separating two plots of land.

The cottage looked like a picture on a chocolate-box, the brasswork on the doorstep gleamed, the diamond-paned windows sparkled. Laurie imagined Mrs Anderson as a small woman bustling with nervous energy.

Ross rang the bell, waited, then rang again. 'Odd.' He looked at his watch. 'Twelve o'clock—I said we wouldn't be any later. I hope she got my message—let's try the back.'

A blue-tit perched on a milk bottle on the back step flew away as they approached, and Ross frowned. 'That's significant. Andy would never leave her milk out for the birds to get at, she's too fearful of germs. Let's take a squint through the window.'

But this revealed nothing but a scrupulously tidy kitchen. The door from it leading to the hall was shut. They tried all the windows after that, but without success, then Ross referred to his watch again.

'She couldn't have gone out; yet if she were in she would have heard us by now. Strange too that the back door is bolted. I've got a strong feeling that something is wrong. Let's try the windows again to see if she's left one unlocked.'

They met again on the back doorstep having worked their way round the cottage without any luck. 'No go, and none of the bedroom windows are open either, so there's no point in looking for a ladder. The only window that's open is that one there,' and Ross pointed to a small square window obviously belonging to a pantry on a level with the top of his head.

'Nobody could get through there, it's too small,' said Laurie dismissively.

He raised his eyebrows at her. 'A little tich like you could manage it easily. Come along, I'll give you a bunk up.' Not giving her a chance to protest, he swung her up into his arms, laughing down at her look of horror.

'I'll never do it—I'll get stuck!'

'You won't get stuck, not if you do as I tell you.'

Once before she had been in his arms like this, the time she had fallen in the ford, but then he had been angry and impatient. Now he looked at her with gleaming, amused eyes, and the closeness of him, the movement of the muscles in his arms filled her with a sensuous longing that made her ashamed. Because of that she held herself as rigid as a post and he laughed again.

'Relax, you little ninny, I won't drop you. Ready—heave—ho—!'

Laurie didn't get stuck, but it was a tight squeeze and didn't do her new skirt any good. At the time though she wasn't thinking about herself but the possible damage she might do to the contents of the pantry. She slid to the ground with no more serious mishap than knocking over a sack of potatoes. Gingerly she felt for the door, the larder was dark—then she was through into the kitchen and light and making for the back door to unlock it for Ross, when she heard a groan.

She was through the other door in a flash, the door that led to the hall, the only room in the house that didn't have a window, and in the gloom she saw the figure of a woman lying huddled at the bottom of the stairs. Her right leg was lying at a grotesque angle, it could be broken—the woman was in her hat and coat as if on her way out. She gave another faint groan, then lapsed into unconsciousness again. Laurie wasted no more time going to fetch Ross.

'What's up?' he demanded as soon as she opened the door.

'It's Mrs Anderson—it looks as if she's fallen down the stairs and broken her leg. Oh, hurry, Ross, I don't like the look of her at all—'

Afterwards she realised she had addressed him by his first name, but at the time neither of them noticed it. Ross hurried past her and into the narrow hallway. There was hardly room for the three of them, Mrs Anderson was by no means a small woman.

Ross felt her pulse, then put his hand inside her coat. 'Her heartbeat is quite strong, considering. She's cold, I think she's been swimming in and out of consciousness for some time. I must get something to cover her up.' He straightened himself. 'I'm trying to think where

I last saw a phone kiosk.'

'There was one at the T-junction.'

'Good girl! You get back there and phone the hospital and ask for an ambulance. Here's the number.' He scribbled on a sheet torn from his diary. 'You can give them my name and say it's urgent—but I don't have to tell you that.' He called after her as she hurried away, 'Take the car, it'll save time.'

Not the way I drive, thought Laurie. She tore up the lane glad that her pleated skirt gave her freedom of movement. Getting through to the hospital was no problem. She blurted out her message, then returned to the cottage, arriving breathlessly just as Ross was making tea.

'This is for you,' he told her.

'What about Mrs Anderson?' queried Laurie.

'No, not if she's to have an anaesthetic. Would you like to go to her while this is brewing?'

Ross had placed a cushion under Mrs Anderson's head and a blanket to cover her. He had improvised a splint and bound it to her leg. Altogether she looked more comfortable than when Laurie had left. The blueness about her lips which had been so frightening was beginning to fade. She opened her eyes when she heard Laurie, and even managed a faint smile.

'I'm sorry to be such a trouble.' Her words were barely audible. 'I wanted to have

211

everything so nice for you. I had bought some sherry, but I'd forgotten the biscuits, and I was just on my way out for them when I fell down the stairs—' She broke off as Ross joined them. 'I was just telling your young lady what a stupid old woman I am, to fall down the stairs like that.'

Ross bent over and took her hand. 'Not stupid, Mrs Anderson, just racing round to have everything perfect as usual. And I'd better introduce you. This is Nurse Bush who's taken Pamela Wakefield's place. You remember Pam, she was at the practice in your time.'

Across the narrow hall Ross's glance caught and held Laurie's, and she could see he was shaking with silent laughter. Obviously Mrs Anderson's use of the words 'your young lady' was causing him secret amusement. Laurie returned his look with a dutiful smile. Not for the world would she let him see that his amusement was her pain.

CHAPTER ELEVEN

It was late afternoon before Mrs Anderson was settled, as comfortably as circumstances allowed, in a side room of the orthopaedic ward of Westbrook Hospital. As she had had nothing to eat or drink since breakfast there had been no delay in getting her to the operating theatre after preliminary examinations in Casualty X-Ray; but she was in the recovery room for two hours, and it was nearly four o'clock before she was taken up to the ward and settled in bed with her leg in traction and an intravenous drip in position. She had come to briefly in the recovery room, but had now drifted back into a drowsy state bordering on unconsciousness. A nurse was in attendance, and Ross felt there was nothing more that he or Laurie could do. He had slipped along to see old Mr Anderson, and to put his mind at rest because the news would soon be out that his wife was in the hospital as a patient just along the corridor. The orthopaedic ward at Westbrook was built to a horseshoe design with the female wards on one side of the semi-circle and the male wards on the other and the nurses' station linking the two. This meant that both medical and nursing staff were common to both wards.

Ross came away with an assurance from Sister that as soon as Mrs Anderson was fully awake her husband would be wheeled in a chair to see her, this being the best medicine for her for the time being, and he went off to the day-room where Laurie was waiting.

She got up and came towards him. 'How is she now?'

He gave the faintest of shrugs. 'If you were a relative asking that you might be given the stock answer—"The operation was successful,

213

the patient has recovered from the anaesthetic and is now sleeping peacefully.'" He spoke in a slightly ironic way which Laurie had once taken for cynicism but now knew was a way of showing his relief.

The fracture was not so bad as he had feared at first sight, but because of her age and her husband's condition it was thought best that Mrs Anderson should be kept in hospital until arrangements at her home could be made. There would have to be a home help of some kind and a nurse—but that was for the future to worry about; now Ross was more concerned about the present and the fact that Laurie had had no lunch. This was not strictly true, they had snatched a cup of coffee and a bite in the staff canteen while waiting for Mrs Anderson to come round after the operation to set her leg. He had phoned the Green Dragon to cancel their booking, but Laurie felt he was still hankering to go on there.

He looked at his watch and pulled a face. 'I'm tied up with the clinic this evening, unfortunately, or I would suggest we stayed on and had dinner out, but I must be back at six-thirty at the latest. I won't have time to show you the sights of Cheltenham, I'm afraid, or even my old school. But I'm determined to salvage something from this outing. We'll see what the Green Dragon can rustle up in the way of tea.'

The old inn was in a village on the far side of

the Spa and there was no reason to go through the town at all, and now that it was dusk there was little for Laurie to see; all the same Ross went that way and pointed out the tall Regency houses visible in the glow of the street lamps. Laurie had an impression of lime-washed façades in soft pastel shades and delicate wrought-iron balustrades enough to fire her enthusiasm for a return visit.

From the outside she couldn't understand why the Green Dragon held such a fascination for Ross. It squatted by the roadside, lit by a row of carriage lamps suspended from crooked beams so lopsided it looked in danger of collapsing in upon itself. But appearances were deceptive—inside all was brightness and comfort. Ross went off to the reception desk to order tea, sending Laurie to the lounge to get warm—the unseasonably warm day now threatened to turn into a bitter night. The lounge was empty but for one woman sitting on a long low settee near the fire with knitting and a pile of magazines beside her. The remains of her tea were on a nearby table. She looked up as Laurie entered and smiled. She was small and slight with silvery coloured hair, perhaps in her middle or late fifties, and her clothes marked her as someone with money. 'It's turned very cold, hasn't it?' she said.

'It's lovely and warm in here, though,' answered Laurie, holding her hands to the blaze. It was the usual exchange of pleasantries between two strangers on neutral ground. Laurel sat down on a corresponding settee on the other side of the fire then turned her attention to her surroundings, while the woman picked up a magazine. The lounge was a long narrow room with a wealth of exposed beams that would have made it gloomy but for the cleverly concealed lighting. A nice touch was the copper baskets filled with hanging plants suspended from many of the beams, and other flowers mostly chrysanthemums, were massed in copper urns at strategic points. There was a lot of brass and copper that gleamed like old gold in the soft light. Laurie made a shrewd guess that the clientele of the Green Dragon did not have to worry about ways and means.

Ross came in, bringing with him a gust of cold air from the outer hall. He was such a large man, so forceful in his masculinity, that he couldn't do anything quietly. The woman looked up with a start, then quickly returned to her magazine. Like Laurie he went straight to the fire to warm his hands. 'This is more like,' he said. He turned and smiled. 'Tea won't be long.' And what a tea it turned out to be—what inducement had Ross used to be served with such a meal at such short notice Laurie wondered? Perhaps just his charm which he could use to good effect when the occasion called for it.

A table was set up before them, ham and tongue sandwiches appeared—muffins in a chafing-dish, scones and jam and cream, and a rich moist fruit cake. 'It's no good considering your figure,' said Ross as Laurie stared. 'In any case, you have no worries on that score—rather the opposite!'

They didn't converse much as they were eating. The warmth, the good food was bringing a sense of drowsiness in its wake, but Laurie was becoming increasingly aware that the woman opposite was watching them covertly while pretending to read. She didn't attach any importance to this, though, as the woman seemed to be more interested in Ross than she was in Laurie she could be a one-time patient. What did strike Laurie about her was the unusual colour of her eyes—they were the nearest to violet she had ever seen. She must have been a very beautiful woman once, now her face was a network of tiny wrinkles as if she had suffered from a long illness or been through a great deal of worry. There were signs of strain about her face even now.

But Laurie soon forgot the woman opposite when Ross suddenly remarked, à propos nothing, 'You should always wear that colour—it suits you.' Prosaic words, but they made her heart sing.

She gave him a provocative smile. 'Shirley was saying the same thing this morning.'

He grunted. 'I always did think that girl had a lot of common sense.' Then he stared broodingly into the fire. Laurie could not help thinking how Ross's compliment differed from the way Nick had compared her eyes to 'azure skies'—but the difference was in the sincerity.

It was her turn to lapse into thought, not all of it pleasant, when Ross aroused her with a teasing, 'A penny for them?'

She shook her head. 'They're worth more than that.'

'One of those new-fangled yellow coins, then.'

'Not even one of those.'

'Very well, keep your thoughts to yourself—only tell me one thing. Am I forgiven for the stupid things I said yesterday?'

Laurie blushed furiously—she had been thinking of just that! Quickly she turned her head, knowing what a giveaway her face could be. 'There's no question of forgiveness,' she blurted out. 'It was the way I reacted—I was too touchy by far. Please, let's not talk about it any more.'

'I just wanted to let you know that I have Nick's New York address if you would like it.'

She faced him then, her eyes wide and guileless. 'There's no question of me ever writing to Nick again or of Nick writing to me. It's all over between us—was weeks ago. I never even give him a thought now. You must believe that.'

She was not to know what Ross's answer to this might have been, for four large men with voices to match suddenly erupted into the

218

room. They were all rubbing their hands and some goodnatured ribaldry was tossed to and fro. They drew chairs up to the fire, making any further private conversation between Laurie and Ross out of the question. A girl came in and they ordered tea—'And none of those fiddling little iced cakes,' one of the men boomed at her. 'I want a thick slab of that black fruit cake with a piece of cheese.'

The woman with the violet eyes also spoke to the girl, then gathered up her books and knitting and left. Two of the men immediately took over the vacant settee.

Ross looked at his watch. I think it's time we were making tracks. I'll take the quick route back, but it will take about forty minutes even so. Had enough to eat?'

'More than enough.'

Laurie tried to keep awake on the return journey, but she kept nodding off and time and again her head lolled sideways to rest on Ross's shoulder. Each time this happened she jerked awake again, until finally he laid his open hand softly on her cheek pressing her head down. 'Don't fight it,' he said. 'If you need sleep, Laurie, then sleep.'

And then almost immediately, it seemed, he was drawing up outside the cottages. As soon as she got out of the car the keen night air stunned her into wakefulness. She looked up. The sky was black and the stars glittered, hard and bright. There was the sharp bite of frost in the air. They had left Merton in sunshine and returned by starlight, and she didn't want this kind of togetherness that had sprung up between them to end. She invited Ross in for a glass of sherry.

He hesitated for a second, then said, 'It will have to be a small one, then—I'd like to change before going to the surgery.'

The cottage was in darkness which meant Shirley was still working. As Laurie switched on the light Kitty stood up in her basket by the fire, arched her back and yawned. Laurie stooped to fondle her, then poked the fire into life, sending a shower of sparks up the chimney. When she looked round again Ross was staring at an unopened letter on the table. Laurie took it in at a glance—the American stamp, the airmail frank, Nick's recognisable handwriting—and her face flooded with colour.

There was a moment of silence between them, fraught by an unfair sense of guilt on her part and on his—what? She could not tell from his face. Then he gave her a keen searching look, and again she felt herself redden.

'Don't bother about the sherry,' he said flatly. 'I'm rushed for time as it is. Thanks all the same.' His words were perfectly civil, yet they hurt more than a calculating insult would have done. She knew he thought she had lied to him about Nick and not being in correspondence with him—the evidence was here, on the table, staring at him. She could have snatched up the hateful letter and thrown it on the fire there and then for the way it had smashed her brief but idyllic happiness, but such a display of histrionics would not have impressed Ross—rather the opposite.

She followed him to the door. He couldn't leave thinking she had lied—she must put that right at least.

But the way she blurted out her excuses only seemed to make matters worse, for Ross only raised his eyebrow in his old sardonic manner and drawled, 'My dear child, why should I be concerned who writes to you? Don't be so upset—it's of no consequence.'

But it was to her. 'I—I wanted to thank you for the—the lovely day—'

'It was *my* pleasure,' he replied with an iciness that stabbed like a knife.

*   *   *

When Shirley came in about fifteen minutes later she was surprised to find Laurie still in her coat staring into the fire. She looked from her to the unopened letter on the table. 'What's up?' she asked.

'That!' Laurie jerked her head at the letter. 'I told Ross that Nick and I were no longer writing to each other—and then we come in here and are confronted by *that*! Now, of course, he believes I lied deliberately.'

221

Shirley gave her friend a searching look. 'Does it matter to you what Ross believes?'

Laurie shrugged her shoulders impatiently. 'Nobody likes to be made to look a fool or a liar.' She suddenly jumped up and snatched the letter, ripped it open and out fell a Christmas card. Silently they both stared at it.

'Pity you didn't open it while Ross was here,' said Shirley matter-of-factly. 'He could have seen how innocuous it is then. It hasn't even got a message in it—just Nick's name.' Her voice softened as she saw Laurie's expression go bleak. 'You do work yourself up about silly little things of no importance. Show it to Ross tomorrow—better still, pin it up in Reception with the others, then everyone can see.'

Laurie did that first thing in the morning, but she didn't see Ross before he went off on his rounds and she was told he was going off to Westbrook Hospital to see the Andersons afterwards. During a quiet period in the afternoon Dr Russett questioned her about the visit to Cheltenham. She had had a detailed account from Ross of Mrs Anderson's accident and the subsequent treatment, but nothing more. She was more interested in the social side of the outing.

It was just what Laurie needed—to talk. A chance to relive those carefree moments in Broadway and in the lounge of the Green Dragon. She waxed so lyrical about the old inn that Rusty could not hide her amusement and egged her on. Actually, she took any opportunity to talk about Ross. She stood there in the middle of her room, her hands deep in the pockets of her cardigan, her hair in its usual disarray, short, sturdy, reliable, her warm brown eyes overflowing with good humour, and it suddenly struck Laurie that all Rusty's enjoyment came secondhand from enjoying the pleasures of others. She had no life outside the surgery, and, what was an even bigger revelation—she didn't want one. These four walls and her flat in Sinclair House—and yes, Ross—this was her life, and her life was by no means empty.

And it was because of this sudden understanding that Laurie began to go into greater details of the outing and even began to describe the woman with the remarkable eyes.

Rusty's square face grew thoughtful. 'Violet eyes?' she queried. 'I knew a woman with violet eyes once—a long time ago. They were beautiful—looked lovely with her black hair.'

'Oh, this one had white hair.'

Rusty shrugged. She stood musing, miles away in thought, then asked casually if Laurie knew whether the woman was staying at the inn, or just having tea there. 'Staying, I'm sure. I heard her tell the waitress she would have dinner in her room.'

Rusty nodded, then picked up her appointments diary and studied it. She thought for a bit and then said she would try and go over to visit Mrs Anderson the following day. Obviously the woman with the violet eyes had gone out of her mind. Julie rang through to say the next patient had arrived and work resumed. There was no more mention of yesterday's outing.

When Ross returned he sought Laurie out in Reception. 'I thought you'd like to know that Mrs Anderson had a good night. She wanted me to give you her kind regards and to thank you for what you did.'

His voice was formal and rather restrained, but that could have been because of Julie's presence. Julie was busy on her ledger, but all ears; as they both knew, not much escaped Julie. The offending card from Nick was pinned up in a prominent place more as a gesture to its unimportance than because it mattered, but Ross didn't even glance at it, much to Laurie's annoyance.

'I didn't do anything,' she said primly.

'You were there when she needed you, and that was everything. She asked me to take you to see her again, but I explained about your exam next week. By the way, I want to see you about that later. Any nuisances for me?' He always referred to messages as nuisances.

'I left them on your message pad.'

'Thanks.' Laurie had the feeling he would have said more but for Julie. When he had gone she felt Julie's eyes on her and tried to keep an impassive expression. But she wasn't

224

very good at it—she hadn't had much practice.

Rusty had her half-day in Cheltenham and came back in an odd frame of mind. She hadn't much to add in her report on the old housekeeper's condition, yet she seemed strangely on edge—a state she remained in for the next two days. Julie said she hovered constantly around Reception as if waiting for a phone call, but the two girls paid little heed to that remark, knowing Julie's fondness for dramatising everything—and in any case the phone rarely stopped ringing, so why wait for it?

Shirley opined that Rusty needed a holiday. She hadn't had one that year, she had been planning to go away in October, but had cancelled her arrangements when Nick left. A replacement for Nick had been advertised for in the *British Medical Journal*, but so far nothing had come of it. It was common knowledge that Ross wanted to appoint someone who had trained at the Eastside, his (and Laurie's) *alma mater*. According to Julie he was due to visit there soon to conduct some interviews.

Shirley wasn't the only one to think Rusty needed a holiday. Ross was even more concerned, and reminded Rusty of her own words: ' "A sick doctor is no good to himself or his patients." Or in this case, herself, so off you go, Rusty, even if it's only for a few days.'

Oddly Rusty, who often refused to take her

free day once a week, put up no objections—
she seemed even pleased to be going away. She
planned to go off the day before Laurie was
due to go to London, easy in mind because
Ross had arranged for an agency doctor to
locum for her. She came to wish Laurie the
best of luck in her exam, and in return Laurie
asked her where she was spending her holiday.

'Not a holiday exactly, just two or three days.
Not far—Cheltenham way—and I'm staying at
the Green Dragon. After the way you cracked
it up to me I tried it out for lunch when I was
there the other day, and it's all that you said it
was and more besides. *And* I shall be near
enough to keep an eye on the Andersons.'

Dear Rusty, Laurie reflected, she couldn't
even take two days away from the surgery
without going on a sort of busman's holiday.

That night Laurie shut herself up in the
deserted surgery and went through her books
for the last time. There was quite a pile of
them—medical books mostly that she had
borrowed from all the doctors. Dr Crowson's
were over forty years old, books he had bought
as a student, but as he said, treatment had
changed but symptoms didn't vary.

Her eyes were beginning to ache with the
effort of concentrating, when the door opened
and Ross came in, taking her by surprise.

'Hallo, still at it!' He looked at the books and
grinned. 'Anatomy—surgery—pathology—
psychology! You're not taking any chances, are

you? How long is this exam—twenty minutes?'

'Twenty minutes is a long time in an examination room,' retorted Laurie quickly, feeling he was laughing at her. The restraint of the past two days had gone and he was back in a bantering mood. She wondered if he had noticed Nick's Christmas card and realised its insignificance. 'Anyway,' she went on, 'I've got to play it safe—I'm out of touch with the syllabus after two years. Goodness knows what they'll cook up.'

'Would you like me to fire some questions at you?' Ross was good at that—he had done it before when they had had some free time together, but she was never at her best then, too aware of the time she had taken her practical before and the effect his slate grey eyes had had on her. Those same eyes were steadily regarding her now, but the greyness was overshadowed by blue streaks.

'You're travelling to London tomorrow, taking your practical Wednesday morning, returning here on Thursday. What are you doing Wednesday afternoon?'

'I thought I might do some Christmas shopping.'

'You couldn't find time to see me, could you?'

She stared, and Ross laughed—a deep-throated chuckle really. 'Don't look so surprised. I'm coming up to the Eastside on Wednesday to interview two applicants for the vacancy here. Just thought I could make up for our lost lunch the other day and take you out to dinner somewhere in Town.'

Laurie's heart leapt with joy—her senses thrilled with delight—yet—yet—Oh, that yet. She couldn't forget the disaster caused by his last visit to the examination room.

He saw the uncertainty in her eyes and gave another low laugh.

'Never fear, Laurie, I promise to keep well away from that side of the hospital. It's just that I thought we'd be company for each other— two lost souls in the wicked city? I'll be staying at my club and I can easily get in touch; you'd better give me your friend's phone number. Anyway, I'll make final plans tomorrow. I'm running you into Chipping Colney, by the way. You're catching the ten-fifteen, aren't you? Right, I'll call for you at quarter to.'

Just like that—at the last minute! She might already have arranged for a taxi or Shirley to take her to the station—but that thought hadn't entered his head. And as Ross knew which train she was catching he must have checked up on her with Julie. The arrogance of the man!—yet she was gratified. She didn't mind that he was no ladies' man and that even his gallantry had its arrogant side. He wouldn't be Ross otherwise.

He called promptly the following morning. Even though Chipping Colney was only four miles from Merton Laurie had never revisited it since her first arrival in the Cotswolds when Nick had met her at the station. Then it had been August, hot and sultry, now it was late November with lowering grey clouds, cold enough for snow.

'Are you wrapped up enough?' asked Ross as they stood on the platform waiting for the train. Laurie was wearing the same outfit she had worn to Cheltenham with a woollen scarf tucked into the collar of her raincoat, and as a concession to the cold a pair of sheepskin mittens she had bought in Merton market. The signal went up and Ross said hastily, 'If by any chance I can't make it on Wednesday I'll phone you—I'll be in touch in any case.' His lean face creased into a lopsided smile and he shook back a lock of hair that had fallen over one eye. 'I'll be thinking of you tomorrow morning and willing you to pass. Any qualms?'

'Not now.' She slipped off one mitt and put her hand into his, and at her touch she saw his eyes darken, and she had one wild moment of rapture when it seemed likely he would he kiss her. But he didn't—he patted her hand, wished her luck, and then she was standing at the window watching the station slide past and taking with her an impression of a tall broad man whose grey eyes held an unfathomable expression.

Nearly three hours later she was in the tiny hall of Sadie's Victorian terrace house being hugged and kissed in welcome. John, ever

229

thoughtful, had made himself scarce so that the two old friends could have this time to themselves. Lunch was ready, but first Laurie had to be taken over the house and shown all the improvements that had been made to it in the past three months. The small room in the front over the porch had been prepared for her; John was redecorating the back bedroom as a nursery and already a chest of drawers was full of baby clothes.

'It's ridiculous, isn't it,' said Sadie, laughing at herself. 'The baby's not due for six months, and here I've got a complete layette already. I can't wait!'

'You were just as bad before you were married,' Laurie remembered. 'Always buying things for what you called your bottom drawer—'

'And a good thing I did too—it's saved a lot of expense since. Goodness knows how we're going to manage when I have to give up work— but I'm not thinking of that now. All I want is to sit with you and talk and talk and talk— we've got about two months' gossip to make up.

*   *   *

Late the following morning Laurie came walking out of Eastside Hospital as if her feet had sprouted wings. She knew she had done well in her practical—she had not only felt it in her bones, she had seen it in the faces of the examiners. As soon as she had stepped into the examination room her adrenalin had started to flow, and from then on she had sailed through. She had to smile ruefully at herself, because she hadn't been asked a single question on any of the subjects she had mugged up—but that didn't matter; just knowing she had mastered them had given her the confidence she needed.

She went on to Oxford Street and did her Christmas shopping, in no hurry to get back to Woodford as Sadie was on duty until six o'clock, then she remembered that Ross might be in London already and trying to contact her, so she made straight for the nearest Underground.

Sadie had given her a spare key. Laurie made herself a sandwich and a cup of tea as soon as she got in; she had skipped lunch, not feeling up to battling with the hordes of shoppers. She felt out of touch with London. It was too big, too crowded and too noisy, though she had enjoyed browsing round the stores admiring the new fashions. But now came the anticlimax, alone in the house waiting for the phone to ring. She began to wonder whether she had given Ross the right number, but he had checked it over with her afterwards as he had written it down. Was the line out of order? She called the exchange—no. Perhaps the interviews were taking longer than Ross had allowed for—perhaps his train had been delayed. Perhaps—perhaps. She was glad when it was time to prepare supper for Sadie and John, it gave her something to do.

Things were better when Sadie came in and she could discuss the exam with her and show her her purchases. Her spirits revived, but as the evening wore on they began to fall again. John had taken himself upstairs to carry on with his decorating and Sadie was sitting with her feet up after a busy day on the ward; her ankles were inclined to swell by evening, so she rested whenever she could. If she noticed Laurie's increasing dejection she made no comment, putting it down to a post-examination reaction. Laurie had been much too excited that morning, and Sadie, with the wisdom of a few years' seniority, had known nothing good would come of it. She got up and went off to make the bedtime drink, refusing Laurie's offer of help.

And then the phone rang. Laurie was across the room before it had the chance to ring twice and snatched up the receiver.

'Hallo—yes, yes—hallo?' she said eagerly.

It was Shirley, ringing to find out how she had got on.

All Laurie's elation left her. 'I'll tell you tomorrow,' she said flatly. 'It's a bit late now.'

'I know. I'm sorry about that, but I've been round to Howard's—I'll tell *you* about that tomorrow too. Actually, I'm surprised to find you in. I thought you might be out on the Town with Ross.'

Laurie gripped the receiver, finding some difficulty with her voice. 'D-did you say Ross?'

'Yes. Isn't he with you? He went off dressed to kill this morning, and I thought anybody dressed like that could only be going to London.'

There was a harrowing pause, then finally Laurie said, 'Well, if he is in Town he isn't with me. I haven't heard from him.'

There was a silence from Shirley's end this time. Then she said, 'Sorry, I've put my big foot in it as usual. It was something Julie said that gave me the idea he'd be in touch with you. I'll meet you tomorrow, then—the midday train? Right, I'll be there.'

She rang off, and Laurie slowly replaced the receiver. Every word Ross had said to her came back to mind as clearly as if she had written it down. 'If by any chance I can't make it on Wednesday I'll phone you—I'll be in touch in any case.' She looked at the clock. Nearly eleven—he wouldn't ring now. It was obvious he had forgotten—or worse still, perhaps he hadn't meant to ring in the first place. He wasn't playing on her feelings, he wasn't that type of a man—but he had the facility of putting anything of no importance clean out of his mind.

She felt her stomach tighten with a nervous ache, then relax as a justified anger took over. 'All right, Dr Ross Cramond,' she muttered through gritted teeth. 'Two can play at that game!'

CHAPTER TWELVE

It was good to be back in the Cotswolds again; two and a half a days in London had been quite enough. It was better still to find Shirley waiting, but not so good to see Fergus in the back of the Fiat, dribbling with excitement in his fever to get at her.

'Oh no!' cried Laurie. 'I'm not in the mood to have a dog slobbering all over my neck!'

'I had to bring him.' Shirley drove out of the station yard and into the Merton road. 'As Ross and Rusty are still away there's no one else to exercise him except for Muggins here. I'll pull into the Coppice on our way back and let him run off his excess energy there.'

The Coppice was a beauty spot and popular picnic area on the Merton to Chipping Colney road, In the spring it was fragrant with bluebells and cowslips, in high summer a pleasant place to linger in to watch the trout basking in the dappled river; but at this time of year when the trees were bare and the trout had the sense to stay in their hatcheries it was too cold to venture out of the car.

Shirley released Fergus and he bounded away, stopping every now and then in his tracks to investigate new smells. He was obedient enough to return to their call, so they had no qualms about letting him run free. Only then did they settle down for a talk.

'So Ross did go off somewhere?' Laurie voiced the thoughts that had occupied her since leaving Chipping Colney.

'Yes, but not to London, as I believed—I'm sorry I jumped to the wrong conclusion about that, though you did mention the possibility. Actually he's gone to Cheltenham—went yesterday with that Marcia Peacock. Julie told me, she saw them driving off together and Matron looking like a "fashion plate"—you know Julie. I don't suppose there's anything in it. They've both got connections in Cheltenham; Ross went to school there and Matron did her training at the hospital.'

'The trip has nothing to do with the Andersons?'

Shirley pursed her lips in thought. 'I doubt it—that's all been settled. Ross has arranged for a home help and a private nurse, and he's footing the bill. He'd do anything for that old couple. But I don't want to talk shop—I want to know how you got on with your exam.'

Laurie was glad to change the subject too. It was bad enough to know that Ross had stood her up without a word of explanation or apology—but on top of that to go off with Matron! She satisfied Shirley's curiosity on the events of yesterday, then it was her turn to ask questions.

'What was it you had to tell me? You sounded very mysterious over the phone.'

A happy little smile flickered over Shirley's mouth. 'I've at last met Robert—Howard's Robert!—*Robert Saunders*,' she explained in exasperation, unaware of the reason for Laurie's lack of attention. 'His school had to close because of an influenza epidemic and the boys who weren't confined to the sanatorium were bundled off home. Howard invited me over yesterday evening to meet him. I can tell you, Laurie, I went off shaking like a leaf, but I got worked up all over nothing. You'll never guess! Master Robert took me off to one side and said very confidentially how pleased he was that his father had found some worthy woman to care for him in his old age. That he, Robert, had been very concerned about the future, feeling that he had no right to a life of his own when he had his father's welfare to consider— but now, what a load it was off his mind. Howard hooted when I told him later—and to think all this time we'd been meeting in secret in case Robert found out and was upset! He's a nice lad, I like him—a bit pompous for a fourteen-year-old, but I'll soon cure him of that.'

'If you can't nobody can,' said Laurie.

'Don't worry, we're going to be good friends, though I must say the thought of being looked upon as a "worthy woman" will take some getting used to!'

Laurie could laugh with Shirley, though her heart was still sore over what she felt was Ross's treachery, and it was because she didn't relish the idea of a long afternoon alone with her thoughts that she went back to the surgery after lunch. Coincidentally Ross and Dr Russett came in soon afterwards. They had just got back from Cheltenham.

As soon as Laurie saw Ross she realised he had undergone some recent traumatic experience. He was masterly at keeping his emotions under control, but he couldn't prevent the nervous throb of a vein in his cheek or disguise the look of ferment in his eyes. All her resentment towards him vanished and she had an illogical yearning to put her arms round him and comfort him. Though he asked politely how she had fared with her exam it was obvious his thoughts were elsewhere, and he made no mention of his broken promises. It was almost as if he had forgotten he had said he would see her in London.

Dr Russett also seemed under a strain, and her eyes looked as if she had been crying. They were puffy and red-rimmed, but she declared she had a cold and kept blowing her nose, though nobody was deceived.

Then for the next few days Laurie had no time to speculate on anything but the work in hand. The influenza epidemic that had closed down Robert Saunders' school now hit

Merton-on-the-Hill. Dr Crowson was heard to remark that he hadn't known anything like it since the Asian 'flu invasion of the fifties. Fortunately the agency doctor was able to stay on until the crisis was over, but even so they were all rushed off their feet.

The epidemic peaked on the third day, then began to subside. The days were becoming steadily colder, with odd flurries of snow giving a threat of what was in store. Laurie began to see less of Ross as now that the work load at the surgery had eased he was spending more time at the hospital, and she could not help wondering and worrying that Marcia Peacock might be the reason.

Christmas was becoming more in evidence. The post arrived later and there was more of it. Julie decorated Reception, and the Christmas tree in the waiting-room became loaded with presents as patients and visitors left offerings that were earmarked for a local children's home.

One day when Laurie slipped across to the cottage to warm up some soup for lunch she found among the pile of cards on the mat two letters addressed to herself. One was from Louise Fellowes, the other an official notification that she had passed her finals and had been awarded the SRN diploma.

At last here it was—the culmination of years of study, of wild dreams and dashed hopes. She was now a qualified nurse! Her main sensation

238

was one of relief. Once, just a few months ago, she would have given the best years of her life to have been able to fling this piece of paper in Ross's face and make him eat his words. Now all she wanted was for him to notice her, to feel pleased for her—but even that seemed too much to ask of him, because ever since he returned from Cheltenham he had been a different man, and she felt excluded from his thoughts.

She opened Louise's letter. It was very short and typical of Louise herself, with sprawling but disciplined writing.

'Did Ross ever mention David Foster to you?' she wrote. 'If he hasn't already done so you're going to hear a lot of him in the future. He's very important to me, Laurie. It's the real thing this time—not a silly girl's infatuation. I won't be home for Christmas after all. Cathy and Frank want me to stay and David won't let me go. I don't think Father will miss me. Tell Ross he wouldn't know me now. The morbid beanpole who used to drape the couch in his private rooms is no more. I've put on nearly a stone!'

Laurie had the opportunity to pass on this message the following morning. It had snowed heavily in the night and those patients who relied on public transport to get to Merton had cancelled their appointments. During a rare but nonetheless agreeably quiet period Laurie took this letter and the one with her results to show Ross. The moment she stepped into his room she realised what a change had come over him. The look of strain had gone from his eyes and mouth and the old sardonic gleam was back in his eyes. She got the full force of it as she handed him the letter from the Royal College of Nursing.

'Congratulations, Laurie—good for you! You'll be celebrating tonight, no doubt?' He lifted one eyebrow questioningly, but she shook her head.

'I haven't got as far as thinking about that yet.'

Ross rose from the desk and came round to where she was standing. He placed his hands on her shoulders and stared down at her with such intensity that her heart began to pound. His touch had such an effect on her that it took all her self-control not to show it. She knew that it would only take the slightest sign from him for her to abandon all pride and fling herself into his arms.

But he made no move and his intent look lapsed into a half whimsical, half serious smile. Laurie could see the bluish streaks in his eyes and from the expression behind them sensed that Ross had reached a significant decision. She closed her eyes, feeling the surge of excitement like a tangible thing gripping them both—then the moment was shattered by the shrilling of the phone.

If he was furious at being interrupted he

didn't show it, though his voice was a little more clipt than usual as he took the call. Laurie heard him say, 'Right, Julie. Tell Matron I'll be over immediately.' He replaced the receiver. When he looked at Laurie again he was wearing his professional face.

'Would you tell Dr Russett I'm wanted urgently at the hospital—it's the hepatitis case—and ask her to cover for me until I get back.' At the door he hesitated with one hand on the handle, looking not at her as much as into the middle distance.

'I'm sorry about this interruption—there was something important I had to say to you, but it will have to wait now. I also wanted to explain why I couldn't make it to London as I promised and to apologise for not letting you know. Rusty will tell you. Tell her from me I want you to know everything.'

He was gone, leaving Laurie to sort out her emotions and try to put her thoughts in order before facing Dr Russett. She discovered her taking a well-earned break with a cup of coffee. She looked up as Laurie entered and said, 'Even a snowfall has its compensations—it's not often I have time on my hands like this. Anything wrong?'

Laurie repeated Ross's words and watched with surprise the different expressions that crossed Rusty's broad face, the chief being a kind of relief. She got up and closed the door as if to prevent any interruption, then returned to

241

her desk, motioning Laurie to the chair opposite.

'Do you remember that first time I went to Cheltenham? When I said I had lunch at the Green Dragon because you recommended it so highly?' She spoke as if choosing her words carefully. 'That was only partly true. I was curious to see the woman you described as having violet-coloured eyes. Do you recall me saying I once knew a woman with eyes the same colour? Call it a hunch, call it a woman's intuition—but I was certain the two women were the same, and I had to find out. I was right. It was Linda Cramond—Ross's mother.'

Laurie was speechless. She stared.

'When you said she couldn't keep her eyes off Ross something clicked—and the rest of the description tallied too, even accounting for a thirty-year gap. And when I walked into the dining-room of the inn, there she was. I recognised her instantly. But I'm afraid she didn't return the compliment.' Rusty permitted herself a wry smile. 'She didn't know me from Eve and was stunned when I identified myself. It wasn't easy at first for either of us—there were too many long-standing prejudices and resentments to break down, but by the time we reached the coffee stage and she had told me her side of the story we'd reached a new understanding.'

It was the old story of a man twenty years older than his wife, set in his ways, unable to meet her halfway in her youthful preferences. He considered a loving husband, a good home, and an infant son were all Linda needed to keep her happy and contented, and couldn't understand her longing to go 'gadding about'. Under the circumstances she could be excused for falling in love with a man her own age and even for running away with him. But very soon afterwards (and this part of the story was new to Rusty) she missed her little boy so much that she wrote to her husband begging to be allowed to come back. He refused. Andrew Cramond was a proud man—proud enough to cut off his nose to spite his face. Through his solicitors he informed his wife that as far as he and *his family* were concerned she was, to all intents and purposes, dead.

'I find it hard to forgive Andrew for that,' said Rusty sadly. 'Foolish man—it warped his life, and look at the effect it had on Ross. He wouldn't grant Linda a divorce either—which virtually prevented her having other children. She and the man she left Andrew for— Geoffrey Bayley—had a happy life together and she remained faithful to him till his death three years ago. He left her very well provided for, though she's a lonely woman. They travelled widely and didn't put down roots anywhere. Since his death Linda's stayed in many different parts of the Cotswolds, drawn back time and again in the wild hope of seeing Ross. She had her methods of finding out about

243

him, she knew what he looked like, what he was doing. Once she came face to face with him while she was staying here in Merton at the White Hart. Of course he didn't know her, but she wouldn't risk coming to Merton again.'

'Didn't she want to make herself known to him?' cried Laurie.

'No. Not like that—not suddenly, anyway. When I met her at the Green Dragon—after I'd talked things over with her and suggested I should get in touch with Ross and arrange for him to join us there—she wouldn't hear of it. She became so distressed I wouldn't press it. I came away feeling I'd served no good purpose at all. I hoped she would change her mind and get in touch with me, but she didn't. I felt if I only had more time with her I might be able to break down the wall of reserve she'd built around herself, so that's why I returned to stay there for a couple of days. She really wanted to see Ross, but she was so frightened of being rejected by him. I phoned him on the Tuesday night to come over—it was too late for him to make the trip that night—but he said he'd be over first thing in the morning, and he was.'

Laurie's mind fastened on one thing—the day Ross had driven over to Cheltenham to meet his mother was the day she had taken her exam. So that was why he hadn't phoned her. She visualised the impact Rusty's call must have made on him, banishing everything else from his mind. Then hard on the heels of this

244

heartwarming reflection came the painful thought, 'But he took Marcia Peacock to Cheltenham with him.'

Just as if she were a thought-reader Rusty said, 'Unfortunately Miss Peacock also had to go to Cheltenham on that day. She phoned Ross to tell him why she wouldn't be at the hospital and he felt obliged to offer her a lift. She was going for an interview for the position of Matron at a private clinic, and I understand she's been offered the job and is taking up her new post after Christmas. But that's beside the point—she didn't know the reason for Ross's business in Cheltenham that day and nobody else knows yet. You realise this is very confidential?'

Laurie realised something even more important as far as she was concerned—that it was just coincidence Ross and Matron going off together. She would like to have believed that the reason for Matron leaving Merton was that she had given up all hope of ever winning Ross—but that was asking too much.

Rusty rubbed her eyes wearily. She looked tired, but the nervous tension she had suffered for the past few days had left her. 'There's no happy ending to this story—not yet anyway,' she said with a faint smile. 'Naturally there was some awkwardness and constraint between Ross and his mother at first, which soon broke down on Ross's part when he learnt her story. But Linda is so bowed down with guilt that she can't even think straight. She won't believe that Ross really wants her to come back, to try and build a new relationship—she thinks he's acting out of a sense of duty, and she won't accept that. She asked for a few days to go away and think things over, and that's how matters were left when we came away. Very unsatisfactory for us all. You must have realised there was something on Ross's mind, and as for me—I seem to be going about like a zombie. All I want for those two is a happy reconciliation—think of all those wasted years! Then this morning Ross heard from her. She's back at the Green Dragon and wants to see him this coming weekend. I hope it means good news. Ross seems to think it does. He looked a much happier man when he told me.'

*　　*　　*

Early after lunch Laurie took the opportunity to go across to Sinclair House and catch up with some of Ross's private work. She wanted a chance to think, and this afforded an opportunity. While her hands were busy addressing accounts and sealing them in envelopes her mind was free to speculate on what Rusty had told her.

She was glad for Ross that there was a chance for him to become reconciled with his mother; she could even feel magnanimous towards Matron now that she was leaving and to wish her well in her new post—a wish qualified by the regret she was not leaving before Christmas rather than after. But her most comforting thought, and one that filled her with a quiet elation, was that Ross wanted her to know about his mother. Surely that signified something?

Then, once again, she was interrupted by the phone. It was Julie.

'I don't know what to do, Nurse,' she sounded harassed. 'Mrs Lomax is on the line. She wanted to speak to Dr Russett, but she's out doing local calls on foot because of the snow and I can't get in touch with her, and Dr Crowson's not back from lunch. Is Dr Ross there?'

'He hasn't returned from the hospital. You'd better put the call through to me.'

Mrs Lomax's voice was shrill with agitation. 'Oh, Nurse Bush, it's you! I'm sorry to be such a worry, but my father's really poorly this time—he can't get his breath properly. I hate to ask anyone to come out on a day like this, but—'

Common sense told Laurie she should immediately ring the hospital and leave a message for Ross, but common sense didn't come into it. Old Mr Burnley had cried wolf too often and she was sure she could deal with any emergency.

'I'll come,' she said promptly. 'Give your father some extra pillows and see that he's propped up. I'll be with you as soon as possible.'

She hurried over to the cottage and changed into warm clothes, pulling boots over her trousers and putting on a body-warmer under her anorak. There was no difficulty getting the Fiat out of the drive, the gardener had cleared the snow earlier.

Laurie found the main roads passable as the snow-ploughs had been out that morning, but the side roads posed a problem. She took the Yaxley road, deciding that the ford would be easier to negotiate than the deep lanes around the Wingfields; all the same her stomach went into a tight knot of apprehension as she approached the river. It was in full spate from recent rains and ice crinkled the edges, only the swift current prevented it from freezing over completely. She took it very slowly, remembering the first time; she did not panic and was over and heading towards Lynch Green, her confidence renewed. The sky was the colour of milk and a glowing red sun hung as if suspended in space without heat and without light. The snow was piled in drifts at the side of the road, and twice she had to get out and shovel it away from the back wheels before she could proceed. She blessed Shirley's foresight at stowing a spade in the boot of the car—but then Shirley had had previous experience of a Cotswold winter.

It was with heartfelt relief that Laurie pulled

up outside Mrs Lomax's cottage. The poor woman was watching for her out of the window, and as soon as Laurie saw her face she realised that this time matters were serious. She was soon hustled up the stairs and into the back bedroom. Mr Burnley was propped up as Laurie had advised and an old-fashioned vaporiser was working on a nearby table. She saw at once that he needed hospital care and the sooner the better. Only now did she regret her foolishness in not contacting Ross.

She had to go to the post office to phone the hospital and got through to Debbie. 'Would you like to speak to Dr Ross?' asked Debbie. 'I'll find him for you—' then she was cut off as another voice interposed. It was Matron, as impervious as ever.

'What's all this about Dr Ross and an ambulance?'

'It's urgent, Matron,' Laurie told her. 'It's old Mr Burnley of Lynch Green. I think he has bronchitis and should be in an oxygen tent—'

'I think you can safely leave a doctor to decide that,' snapped Matron sarcastically.

'Then I'll wait with Mr Burnley until the ambulance arrives.'

'You'll do no such thing.' Matron was frosty. 'His daughter is with him? She knows how to cope, so there's no point in you hanging around wasting time. I'm sure you can find something to do at the surgery!' There was a sharp click as she hung up. As far as she was concerned that was the end of the matter.

Laurie trudged back through the snow thinking things about Marcia Peacock not suitable to be spoken aloud. Had the woman any idea of weather conditions? Did she know what the roads were like? Not likely—cossetted in that central-heated hospital, and now there was no chance of getting a lift back with the ambulance.

Mrs Lomax was equally indignant and wouldn't allow Laurie to leave until she had had a hot drink, and while she was sipping Laurie pondered on the best way back. The more direct route was through the ford at Yaxley, but that was the way the ambulance would take, and she couldn't take the risk of meeting that head-on and impeding its progress. The only alternative was through Lower Wingfield—a deep valley and a sure trap for snowdrifts, but she would have to chance that.

Daylight was fading, the sun had dipped below the horizon and ominous clouds had piled up in the west. Laurie made slow, tiring progress, driving in low gear until she came to a point where the snow had drifted into a solid wall blocking the road. There was no question of shovelling her way out of that. She cut the engine and got out of the car, losing her foothold on the frozen snow. There wasn't a house to be seen; there was nothing but acres of snow and skeletal trees casting long blue

250

shadows. The silence was uncanny and she had the eerie sensation that she was the last human being on earth. She knew the wisest thing was to stay in the car, but it might be hours before help came and in that time she could freeze to death. She felt better doing something active and started on her way back, forcing a foothold in the tracks left by the Fiat. She lost count of the numbers of times she fell. On the last occasion she felt too exhausted to rise again, she was so weary and so cold. All she wanted was to curl up and sleep—but she was alert to the dangers of doing that. And then she saw, making slow desperate progress two beams of light, like the eyes of some prehistoric animal, coming towards her.

It was a car—it was rescue! Laurie struggled to her feet and stumbling, shouting, feebly waving, went to meet it. Her legs buckled under her and she was gasping and floundering in the snow when she was aware that the car had stopped beside her, and then someone swooped on her and gathered her up into powerful arms, her frozen face was pressed against Ross's warm cheek and she was laughing and crying and hugging him round his neck and telling him quite unashamedly how much she loved him.

He put her in the back of the car and sitting beside her cocooned her in a blanket and forced fiery liquid down her throat. She coughed and spluttered, but it did the trick—

warmth coursed over her body and the stultifying effect the cold had had on her senses slowly dispersed. With a clearer mind came the realisation of how blatantly she had revealed her feelings.

In the dim light she could see the gleam of his eyes, but not the expression in them—her imagination could fill that in. He would have that quizzical half-sardonic look, wondering what latent passion he had awakened in this small creature he had plucked out of the snow—and she didn't care! She felt no awkwardness, no shyness, only a blessed thankfulness that she was safe in Ross's arms and that he knew she loved him.

His laugh when it came was rich with humour and gladness. 'And I thought you hated me! You made a good job of showing it when you first arrived at Merton. What was it you called me, my precious Laurie? An ill-natured, arrogant bore—'

She freed one hand and placed her fingers against his lips. 'Please don't remind me what an idiot I was. I thought I hated you—but oh, Ross, it couldn't have been hate, not really. I don't think I know what hatred really is. It's just a word.'

'Do you know what love is?' he said softly. 'Or will I have to teach you?'

His words sent a quiver of sweet anticipation through her and she surrendered to his passion as his lips, ardent and demanding, sought hers.

She didn't have to ask him to declare his love—Ross was a man of action not words. Breathlessly she broke free when she felt control slipping away. There were certain things that had to be cleared up first, misunderstandings to be put an end to. There was Matron, for instance—but as soon as she mentioned her Ross exploded with wrath.

'That blasted woman—I'd like to wring her neck! Mrs Lomax told me about you being ordered back to the surgery and the way you were going. I only waited to see her father safely in the ambulance and then I came after you. Thank God Marcia Peacock won't be queening it over the hospital much longer!'

'And I thought you were attracted to her. You seem to have spent more time at the hospital lately—'

Ross's arms tightened around her and she heard him give a low, delighted chuckle. 'How it boosts my ego to know I can make you jealous—it gives me a very satisfying power over you, my love.' He softened his words by a tender kiss. 'My trips to the hospital have had nothing to do with Matron—though the fact of her leaving has caused some administrative problems which need clearing up. No, it's a busy time at the hospital just now, making plans for the Christmas festivities. My father started the tradition of supplying the turkeys and I've carried it on. The catering supervisor waylaid me just as I was leaving, and thank God he did, because Debbie saw me and passed on your message and I came straight out to Lynch Green.'

It had started to snow again. Cradled in Ross's arms watching the snowflakes dancing in the light of the car's headlamps, Laurie felt as if she had come into safe harbour. 'When did you realise you loved me, Ross?' she asked.

'I don't think I did realise it fully until today. I only knew that you had a powerful impact upon me from that first moment I saw you in Eastside Hospital. You stood there in that interview room with your huge blue eyes and masses of black hair, and I had a sudden vision of my mother as she was at your age. I tried to blot you out of my mind, but I couldn't. I thought I detested all women—but I didn't. I was warped in my opinions, but you cured me of that, you little blue-eyed witch.'

Mention of his mother roused Laurie. 'What's going to happen now, Ross?' she asked.

'Did Rusty tell you about the letter I received this morning? She did. I want you to come with me to see her, Laurie. We must both try to persuade her to come back to Merton. After all, she'll be gaining a daughter-in-law as well as a son.'

It was not the most romantic of proposals, but that didn't matter to Laurie. The only thing that mattered was that never again would misunderstanding be allowed to come between

254

her and Ross. She stirred in his arms, gazing at him with loving eyes. 'I don't really want to move,' she said, 'I'm so happy like this, but don't you think we ought to try and get back.'

Ross gave one of his low amused laughs. 'Look, Laurie—it's snowing again, hadn't you noticed? We'll never make our way through this. We'll have to stay put until the snowplough rescues us, and that might not be until morning.'

Laurie relaxed and he caught the whisper of a contented sigh. As he crushed her against him seeking her lips, he heard her say, 'Oh, darling Ross—Matron didn't plan this!'

We hope you have enjoyed this Large Print book. Other Chivers Press or G.K. Hall & Co. Large Print books are available at your library or directly from the publishers.

For more information about current and forthcoming titles, please call or write, without obligation, to:

Chivers Press Limited
Windsor Bridge Road
Bath BA2 3AX
England
Tel. (01225) 335336

OR

G.K. Hall & Co.
P.O. Box 159
Thorndike, Maine 04986
USA
Tel. (800) 223-2336

All our Large Print titles are designed for easy reading, and all our books are made to last.